The Garden of Dreams

Ruskin Bond is known for his signature simplistic and witty writing style. He is the author of several bestselling short stories, novellas, collections, essays and children's books; and has contributed a number of poems and articles to various magazines and anthologies. At the age of twenty-three, he won the prestigious John Llewellyn Rhys Prize for his first novel, *The Room on the Roof*. He was also the recipient of the Padma Shri in 1999, Lifetime Achievement Award by the Delhi Government in 2012 and the Padma Bhushan in 2014.

Born in 1934, Ruskin Bond grew up in Jamnagar, Shimla, New Delhi and Dehradun. Apart from three years in the UK, he has spent all his life in India, and now lives in Landour, Mussoorie, with his adopted family.

RUSKIN BOND
The Garden of Dreams

RUPA

Published by
Rupa Publications India Pvt. Ltd 2022
161-B/4, Gulmohar House,
Yusuf Sarai Community Centre,
New Delhi 110049

Sales centres:
Bengaluru Chennai
Hyderabad Kolkata Mumbai

Copyright © Ruskin Bond 2022

All rights reserved.
This is a work of fiction. Names, characters, places and incidents are either the product of the author's imagination or are used fictitiously and any resemblance to any actual person, living or dead, events or locales is entirely coincidental.

No part of this publication may be reproduced, transmitted, or stored in a retrieval system, in any form or by any means, electronic, mechanical, photocopying, recording or otherwise, without the prior permission of the publisher.

P-ISBN: 978-93-5520-767-8
E-ISBN: 978-93-5520-768-5

Second impression 2025

10 9 8 7 6 5 4 3 2

The moral right of the author has been asserted.

Printed in India

This book is sold subject to the condition that it shall not, by way of trade or otherwise, be lent, resold, hired out, or otherwise circulated, without the publisher's prior consent, in any form of binding or cover other than that in which it is published.

CONTENTS

Introduction   vii

1. The Garden of Dreams   1
2. Braving Mussoorie's Madding Crowd   11
3. The Kitemaker   14
4. Toria and the Daughter of the Sun   19
5. Boyhood Dreams   24
6. Children of India   38
7. Up the Spiral Staircase   44
8. Bus Stop, Pipalnagar   51
9. A Long Walk for Bina   80

INTRODUCTION

When we are young our dreams know no bounds. We are full of unbridled optimism and believe everything to be possible. As we grow older, it gets harder and harder to hold on to hopefulness. And yet, it is in the nature of human beings to hope—against evidence, against proof, against our better judgement.

So what helps us keep our dreams alive? Often it's the memory of our youthful uninhibited optimism. We think of the ten-year-old that put on shows for her parents in hopes of one day dancing for an audience; we think of the sixteen-year-old who hoped of leaving her small town and had great ambitions for her city life; we think of the joy, the laughter, the energy this dreaming brought us.

This book is a collection of such stories; some real, some aspirational, some fictional that help the child in us stay alive and kicking. It tells us of the friendships we form that help us dream bigger, that carry us when all is lost; it tells the tale of an old man who once made a kite so beautiful that the light of the memory still brings him delight; its tells us the tale of love and romance, and how no matter how old you get, new love can make you giddy like it does to teenagers. This is a book that advocates for hoping against hope.

Ruskin Bond

THE GARDEN OF DREAMS

It wasn't so long ago that I found myself in Kathmandu, the colourful capital of Nepal, attending one of those literary festivals that have caught on in countries where books are still written, published and sometimes read. I had a day or two to myself, and I was wandering about in the streets looking for quaint corners—for I am a collector of quaint corners—when I came across a walled enclosure, a long high wall with just an entrance, a heavy door over which was painted the following legend: 'Garden of Dreams'.

Naturally, I was curious. If there was a garden it was behind that wall. And since it had advertised itself, presumably it was open to the public.

On the pavement, not far from the entrance, sat an old woman who was selling trinkets, costume jewellery and semi-precious stones.

'Mother,' I said, for she seemed older than me, 'What's in that Garden of Dreams?'

'Flowers,' she said, 'And running water. And dreams.'

Her face was furrowed with the passage of time, but she had a cheerful, winning smile and her forearms were covered with the colourful bangles, her fingers with rings of onyx and jade.

'I suppose I can go in,' I said.

'It will open any minute,' she said. 'But first, why don't you buy something? A bracelet for your lady-love?'

'I don't have a lady-love.' But I bought a tiny mirror from her. It was ringed with different coloured stones and crowned with a gaudily painted wooden parrot. As I pocketed my purchase, the door to the garden opened, and the old lady said, 'You can go in now and look for your dream.'

There was no one at the door, and I couldn't see anyone in the garden, although there were signs of activity at the other end, where a couple of gardeners were pruning a rose bush.

There were roses everywhere—lush golden roses, and pink lollipops, and roses that opened like a woman's labia, and roses that shone in the early morning sun, and some that still held dewdrops between their petals.

I had the garden to myself for almost half an hour, and in that time, I followed little paths that meandered between beds of crimson poppies, scented petunias of every shade, carpets of multicoloured phlox, pansies with their funny faces that looked like Oliver Hardy's larkspur, wallflowers, snapdragons…

There was a small waterfall at one end of the garden and it fed a small stream that ran in and out of the spaces between the flower beds. Here and there you could cross the stream by means of small bridges. They gave the garden a distinct Japanese or Oriental look.

I sat down on a bench and tried to take it all in. I am a sensualist by nature, but here there was so much to absorb—colour, fragrance, sunshine and shade, the flow of water, the pattern of leaves, the twitter of small birds, the passage of a butterfly…. And presently, other people were trickling into the garden—some Japanese tourists, laden with cameras; a stout Indian lady in a pink sari, accompanied by a brood of children; a bearded, bespectacled artist with a sketch pad; an English-looking woman lurking beneath a large hat.

The woman in the hat stopped beside me and said, 'Lovely garden, isn't it? So very English…'

'They say the late Rana was inspired by a garden he saw in France,' I commented.

'But French gardens are so formal, aren't they? And this one has something of everything. Even a bit of the willow pattern plate. Was that Chinese or Japanese?'

'Probably a bit of both,' I said. 'Let's just say it's uniquely Nepalese!'

The lady in the hat moved on, and the woman in the pink sari plonked herself down on the bench. She was soon joined by two of her noisy children, and I made way for them and strolled across to the far end of the garden. Here, a fountain was playing, and in the pool surrounding it, there were several goldfish. Nearby there was a girl on a swing. She could have been sixteen or twenty-six, I couldn't guess her age, she was young and pretty, but she was also quite adult in her poise and manner. She made me think of *Alice in Wonderland*. She was dressed all in green, but there was a purple hibiscus in her hair.

'Do you like goldfish?' she asked.

'I do,' I said. 'There is something very restful about them. I can watch them for hours. How they silently glide around in their watery world.'

'And they don't bark,' she said. 'Or make any noise at all.'

I laughed. 'Do you come here often?'

'Quite often,' she said. 'It's your first visit, isn't it?'

'Yes, and I'm only here for a day or two. This garden belonged to a princess, I'm told. Does anyone live there now, in the old palace?'

'Sometimes the princess comes. But she's very old now—she doesn't come down from her tower.'

'And you—are you a princess too?'

She laughed, and I noticed that her eyes were dark like hazelnuts. There were silver anklets on her feet and a daisy chain around her throat.

'No,' she said, 'I'm just a—' She broke off and looked away and there was a touch of sadness on her face. 'I do all sorts of things,' she said, sounding quite cheerful again. 'Have you seen the birds?'

'You mean the sparrows?'

'No, the aviary. There are lots of small birds. Come, I'll show you.'

She jumped off the swing and beckoned, and I found myself by her side, holding her hand.

Had she taken my hand or had I taken hers? I wasn't sure. It was just something that had happened.

The touch of her hand sent a strange thrill through my entire person. It wasn't like any hand that I'd ever held. It was a young hand, the palms soft and the fingers strong; but it was also the hand of her ancestors, and I felt that it had stories to tell. It was also taking something out of me. I felt younger, even reckless. I clung to her hand as though I was clinging to life itself; I did not want to let go.

A variety of small, colourful birds flitted about the spacious aviary, some on swings, some on the branches of a small blossoming plum tree. Plum blossoms were flung far and wide. There was a great amount of birdsong, if you could call it that. Really just twittering and chirping, like a bunch of cocktail party humans having a gossip session. A pair of lovebirds appeared to be enamoured of each other; they kept kissing each other with their tiny beaks.

'See, they are making love!' exclaimed my companion, her

hand pressing into mine. Her hazel eyes were excited. I was tempted to kiss her, but at that moment, the large-hatted lady loomed over us and we became self-conscious.

'Sexy little creatures, aren't they?' she said. 'Just like a couple of teenagers.'

She was obviously referring to the lovebirds, for I was no teenager; but my companion led me away, still holding me by the hand.

She took me into a shady arbour, and we sat there for some time, and she told me her name, Kiran, and that she lived close by and came to the garden almost every day. I did not ask her too many questions. Conscious that I was much older than her and that she knew nothing about me, I did not want to frighten her off with too much familiarity. A gazelle will come to you if you are very still, but if you move towards it, the beautiful creature will dart away. And this was a gazelle I was talking to.

She asked me questions, and I told her about myself—that I worked for an Indian publishing firm and that I was in Kathmandu for a few days—with just a day or two to go.

'Will you come again tomorrow?' she asked.

'If you like,' I said, 'And then perhaps you can show me the marketplace. It's close by, isn't it?'

'Yes, quite close. But I like it here in the garden.' She had released my hand, and I felt that something was going from me. And then the lady in the pink sari barged in with her kids and the spell was broken.

She walked with me as far as the garden door. I looked back at the tall, old building behind the garden.

'Do you live there?' I asked.

She nodded, smiling wistfully.

'It looks very old,' I said. 'So you really are a princess?'

She laughed and her dark eyes lit up in the sunshine. 'I am anything I want to be.'

'Till tomorrow, then,' I said.

'Till tomorrow...'

And so we parted. Out on the street, I bought another trinket, and the old lady noticed that I looked happy and she gave me a toothless grin and asked, 'Did you find your dream?'

'Better than a dream,' I said and made my way back to the hotel where I had a meeting with local publishers.

♦

I forget how I spent the rest of that day. I kept thinking about the girl in the garden. We had struck up a good rapport, and I wanted to see her again and take our friendship forward.

So next morning, after breakfast, I sallied forth to the Garden of Dreams.

She wasn't there.

I walked around the garden several times. I hung about near the pool and the aviary, and sat on a bench for at least an hour. Visitors came and went. Tourists from China and Japan—talking, admiring. Loud-voiced Americans. Some quiet, reserved Africans. A writer from India came up to me and thrust a folder into my hands. 'For you to publish,' he said. 'It will sell in millions!' He must have followed me into the garden. I promised to read his masterpiece.

Then I paced about, studying rose bushes, herbaceous borders, lovebirds. No one came.

It was getting on to noon when I gave up and left the garden.

No, I did not buy any trinkets.

The old woman looked up at me and said, 'No good dream today?'

I shook my head and said, 'Yesterday I met a girl in the garden. She said her name was Kiran. She was to meet me again today. She was a princess, I think. Do you know her?'

The old woman shook her head. 'There is no princess living here. Kiran? I do not know the name. Perhaps she could not come today. Why not try tomorrow?'

'But I must leave tomorrow.'

'It is sad, then. She means much to you, this girl?'

'I think so.'

She nodded wisely. 'Many hearts have been broken in the Garden of Dreams.' And she said no more.

◆

I wandered the streets of Kathmandu. I wasn't looking for anyone. I just couldn't stand being alone in my hotel room or in the company of writers and publishers.

Towards evening, I passed the Garden of Dreams. The door was shut, the walls were too high to see anything. I supposed she did not want to see me again. That overture of friendship, the pressure of her hand, the tenderness in her eyes, her every gesture had spoken of liking, if not love. Perhaps it meant nothing after all. Just a way of passing the time.... And here I was, a middle-aged moron, fretting like an adolescent who had just fallen in love!

My plane was to leave at noon.

There was time for one last visit to the garden, albeit a hurried one.

It was far too early. The street was deserted. The garden door was locked from within. The old lady with her wares was yet to arrive. The sun was only just coming up.

Further along the street, where the garden enclosure ended,

someone was sweeping the pavement using a long-handled broom. Fallen leaves and plastic waste were being swept into an imposing heap—all so symbolic of the new century.

I approached the early morning sweeper. Perhaps he could help me.

It wasn't a 'he'. The person, dressed in a uniform of sorts, turned to me when I spoke, and I was shocked into silence, for it was none other than Kiran.

She was as surprised as I was. She dropped the broom. A look of panic crossed her face and then vanished just as quickly.

'You are here—so early—it does not open till ten.'

'I came to see you, not the garden,' I said. 'And you promised to meet me yesterday.'

'I could not come. I was sent into town on some work. My father works for the old king's family. But as you can see, I am not a princess. That was just a game.' She gave me an enigmatic smile.

'So let the game continue,' I said and held out my hand.

She took it, held it for a moment, then let it fall. 'You are a good person,' she said simply.

'And you are a princess,' I said, 'And I want to see you again. But my plane leaves shortly. If I come again in a few months' time, will you be here?'

'In the garden or outside?' Her good humour was returning.

'Near the aviary. Where the lovebirds sing.'

'They don't sing,' she said, laughing. 'They kiss each other all the time.'

Well, I didn't kiss her, although I longed to do so. The street was filling up, people were staring at us. There were no cell phones then, but I gave her my home address and asked her to write to me. Then I rushed back to the hotel, collected my bag, sent for a taxi and headed for the airport.

Soon the garden and Kiran were just a dream.

◆

But it was a dream that wouldn't go away.

The monsoon rains came and went, and an autumn breeze swept across the hills and knocked over the windows of my hilltop home. There was no word from Kiran. Perhaps she did not write letters. Perhaps she did not write at all!

On my desk was the little mirror I'd bought from the old lady outside the garden. It sparkled in the morning sun; it glowed at the time of sunset. A little bird—just a sparrow—flew in at the open window—examined the wooden parrot, pecked at the mirror and flew away. Sometimes I thought I saw someone in the mirror—just a figure, a slight figure in green, but she was always walking away. Mirrors can play tricks.

And this planet, this earth and its hidden fires, can be cruel.

An earthquake struck the Himaal.

It ran through the heart of Nepal, razing towns, villages, palatial buildings and humble dwellings. Thousands perished. Thousands lost their homes, their living, their loved ones. These sudden horrific natural calamities almost always strike the poorest, most vulnerable countries—Haiti, Mozambique, small island nations, landlocked mountain-lands, Nepal...

As the news came through on my television, I feared the worst. Would Kiran have survived? And what of other friends and associates? I phoned them, made enquires, but news trickled through very slowly. People were too busy salvaging what was left of their homes. And many slept in the open as aftershocks ran through the country, bringing down structures already weakened by the earth's convulsions.

And then there was a period of quiet as things began to settle. Normalcy could not return, but the resilient people of this small nation went about rebuilding their homes and shattered lives.

There was no news of Kiran or the garden or the old lady on the street. They were not people who normally made the news. I would have to visit Kathmandu again, to see if the garden and its occupants were still there.

But before I could do that, I had a visitor.

The steps to my room are steep and uneven, and I was struggling up them after a visit to the bazaar when I noticed someone sitting on the top step, a backpack by her side.

It was Kiran. She looked tired and weak, but more beautiful than ever.

'I've come to see you,' she said.

'For a long, long time, I hope.' And I took her by the hand and led her into my home, my garden of books.

And that was how Kiran came into my life.

If you meet her, she will tell you about the garden of dreams (it's still there) and the old lady on the street (she's still there) and the lovebirds and the goldfish and the little stream. And perhaps she will take you there some day, for she is a girl who can make dreams come true.

BRAVING MUSSOORIE'S MADDING CROWD

It's mid-season in Mussoorie, and I am fighting my way down the Mall road along with thousands of tourists, holidaymakers and locals, determined to enjoy the delights of the hill station. The car could make no progress, having been rammed into a pram. Fortunately the pram was empty. But as we could make better progress on foot, we abandoned the car and joined the happy throng.

Pram-pushers do good business at this time of the year, as frazzled mothers soon tire of lugging their babies around on the Mall. When my royalties dry up, I shall get a pram and make a living pushing babies around. It's easier than driving a taxi.

The destination is the Savoy, where I am to lunch with Shubhadarshini, who made a TV serial called 'Ek Tha Rusty' many years ago. Since then, we have both grown older and wiser.

The crowd increases as I near Gandhi Chowk or Library Bazaar, as it is known to the locals. Here, the wayside vendors are busy, selling everything from balloons and candyfloss to boiled eggs and roasted peanuts. I am persuaded to buy a boiled egg. They even peel it for me and provide me with a generous amount of salt and pepper. The pepper gets up my nose, and I start sneezing so vigorously that the crowd parts, making my progress easier.

After manoeuvring past the traffic jam at Gandhi Chowk, I finally reach the Savoy. Sanctuary! Its extensive grounds and garden give me a feeling of unfettered freedom. And I am welcomed like an old friend, for this was a favourite watering place in the old days.

I am welcomed to the Writers' Bar, given a gin and tonic, then led in a procession to the dining room, where I am served a Shepherd's Pie, my favourite dish. The management refuses to let us pay for lunch. They are not sure if I'm real, or the returning spirit of one of those famous writers whose names are commemorated on the wall of the Writers' Bar. But I look substantial enough, more flesh than spirit, and the Shepherd's Pie finds its true home.

Two hours later, I am on the Mall again, walking a little unsteadily in the direction of home and hearth. A cycle rickshaw is summoned. I pour myself into it, relax like an overfed sloth bear. The rickshaw barely moves, the crowd is so dense.

A large lady keeps pace with the rickshaw. She is holding a baby in her arms.

'Can you hold the baby for a little while?' she asks, and before I can refuse, she has dumped her infant into my arms. The child does its best to remove my spectacles.

'Where are you from?' I ask the mother. 'Amritsar,' she says, 'You must come to Amritsar.'

I promise to come. When royalties run out, I can make a living as a babysitter in Amritsar. After some time, she takes the baby back and disappears into a beauty parlour.

Ships that pass in the night...

Finally, I arrive at the bookshop. No one is buying books today, although some kids are looking at the colouring books on the pavement and dripping ice cream all over them. It's a hot day, and ice creams have priority over books.

Someone from the crowd recognizes me, walks over and thrusts a hundred-rupee note into my hand. 'Well, thank you very much,' I say. 'That's extremely generous of you.'

'No, no !' he says. 'I want your autograph. On the note, please.'

'But is that legal?' I ask, longing to hang on to the note.

'Of course. The RBI Governor has signed it. Gandhiji's photo is on it. You have their blessings. Please sign.'

'Wouldn't you prefer an autographed book? Only sixty rupees.'

'No, I only collect notes. See, I have one autographed by John Abraham.'

Flattered to be in such starry company, I gave him my autograph. Then I bought a colouring book. Colouring it would be therapy of a sort. Better than reading gory American crime novels.

The owner of the bookstore refused to take any payment for the colouring book. Instead, he suggested that I author colouring books. They sold better than books that had to be read.

And finally I stumbled home and went to bed.

Not a bad day, after all. Shepherd's Pie at the Savoy. A gin and tonic. A free colouring book. My autograph in demand—and that too, beside the RBI Governor's. And an invitation to Amritsar to be a babysitter.

Never a dull moment on an author's day off.

THE KITEMAKER

There was but one tree in the street known as Gali Ram Nath—an ancient banyan that had grown through the cracks of an abandoned mosque—and little Ali's kite was caught in its branches. The boy, barefoot and clad only in a torn shirt, ran along the cobbled stones of the narrow street to where his grandfather sat nodding dreamily in the sunshine in their back courtyard.

'Grandfather,' shouted the boy. 'My kite has gone!'

The old man woke from his daydream with a start and, raising his head, displayed a beard that would have been white had it not been dyed red with mehendi leaves.

'Did the twine break?' he asked. 'I know that kite twine is not what it used to be.'

'No, Grandfather, the kite is stuck in the banyan tree.'

The old man chuckled. 'You have yet to learn how to fly a kite properly, my child. And I am too old to teach you, that's the pity of it. But you shall have another.'

He had just finished making a new kite from bamboo, paper and thin silk, and it lay in the sun, firming up. It was a pale pink kite, with a small green tail. The old man handed it to Ali, and the boy raised himself on his toes and kissed his grandfather's hollowed-out cheek.

'I will not lose this one,' he said. 'This kite will fly like a bird.' And he turned on his heels and skipped out of the courtyard.

The old man remained dreaming in the sun. His kite shop was gone, the premises long since sold to a junk dealer; but he still made kites, for his own amusement and for the benefit of his grandson, Ali. Not many people bought kites these days. Adults disdained them, and children preferred to spend their money at the cinema. Moreover, there were not many open spaces left for the flying of kites. The city had swallowed up the open grassland that had stretched from the old fort's walls to the riverbank.

But the old man remembered a time when grown men flew kites and great battles were fought, the kites swerving and swooping in the sky, tangling with each other until the string of one was severed. Then the defeated but liberated kite would float away into the blue unknown. There was a good deal of betting, and money frequently changed hands.

Kite flying was then the sport of kings, and the old man remembered how the Nawab himself would come down to the riverside with his retinue to participate in this noble pastime. There was time, then, to spend an idle hour with a gay, dancing strip of paper. Now everyone hurried, in a heat of hope, and delicate things like kites and daydreams were trampled underfoot.

He, Mehmood the kitemaker, had, in the prime of his life, been well known throughout the city. Some of his more elaborate kites once sold for as much as three or four rupees each.

At the request of the Nawab, he had once made a very special kind of kite, unlike any that had been seen in the district. It consisted of a series of small, very light paper disks trailing on a thin bamboo frame. To the end of each disk, he fixed a sprig of grass, forming a balance on both sides. The surface of the foremost disk was slightly convex, and a fantastic face was painted on it, having two eyes made of small mirrors. The disks, decreasing in size from head to tail, assumed an undulatory form and gave the kite the appearance of a crawling serpent. It required great skill to raise this cumbersome device from the ground, and only Mehmood could manage it.

Everyone had heard of the 'Dragon Kite' that Mehmood had built, and word went round that it possessed supernatural powers. A large crowd assembled in the open to watch its first public launching in the presence of the Nawab.

At the first attempt, it refused to leave the ground. The disks made a plaintive, protesting sound, and the sun was trapped in the little mirrors, making the kite a living, complaining creature. Then the wind came from the right direction, and the Dragon Kite soared into the sky, wriggling its way higher and higher, the sun still glinting in its devil eyes. And when it went very high, it pulled fiercely at the twine, and Mehmood's young sons had to help him with the reel. Still the kite pulled, determined to be free, to break loose, to live a life of its own. And eventually it did so.

The twine snapped, the kite leaped away towards the sun, sailing on heavenward until it was lost to view. It was never found again, and Mehmood wondered afterwards if he had made too vivid, too living a thing of the great kite. He did not make another like it. Instead, he presented to the Nawab a musical kite, one that made a sound like a violin when it rose into the air.

Those were more leisurely, more spacious days. But the Nawab had died years ago, and his descendants were almost as poor as Mehmood himself. Kitemakers, like poets, once had their patrons; but now no one knew Mehmood, simply because there were too many people in the gali, and they could not be bothered with their neighbours.

When Mehmood was younger and had fallen sick, everyone in the neighbourhood had come to ask after his health; but now, when his days were drawing to a close, no one visited him. Most of his old friends were dead and his sons had grown up—one was working in a local garage and the other, who was in Pakistan at the time of the Partition, had not been able to rejoin his relatives.

The children who had bought kites from him 10 years ago were now grown men, struggling for a living; they did not have time for the old man and his memories. They had grown up in a swiftly changing and competitive world, and they looked at the old kitemaker and the banyan tree with the same indifference.

Both were taken for granted—permanent fixtures that were of no concern to the raucous, sweating mass of humanity that surrounded them. No longer did people gather under the banyan tree to discuss their problems and their plans; only in the summer months did a few seek shelter from the fierce sun.

But there was the boy, his grandson. It was good that Mehmood's son worked close by, for it gladdened the old man's heart to watch the small boy at play in the winter sunshine, growing under his eyes like a young and well-nourished sapling putting forth new leaves each day. There is a great affinity between trees and men. We grow at much the same pace, if we are not hurt or starved or cut down. In our youth, we are resplendent creatures, and in our declining years, we stoop a little, we remember, we stretch our brittle limbs in the sun, and then, with a sigh, we shed our last leaves.

Mehmood was like the banyan, his hands gnarled and twisted like the roots of the ancient tree. Ali was like the young mimosa planted at the end of the courtyard. In two years, both he and the tree would acquire the strength and confidence of their early youth.

The voices in the street grew fainter, and Mehmood wondered if he was going to fall asleep and dream as he so often did, of a kite so beautiful and powerful that it would resemble the great white bird of the Hindus—Garuda, God Vishnu's famous steed. He would like to make a wonderful new kite for little Ali. He had nothing else to leave the boy.

He heard Ali's voice in the distance but did not realize that the boy was calling him. The voice seemed to come from very far away.

Ali was at the courtyard door, asking if his mother had returned from the bazaar. When Mehmood did not answer, the boy came forward repeating his question. The sunlight was slanting across the old man's head, and a small white butterfly rested on his flowing beard. Mehmood was silent; and when Ali put his small brown hand on the old man's shoulder, he met with no response. The boy heard a faint sound, like the rubbing of marbles in his pocket.

Suddenly afraid, Ali turned and moved to the door, and then ran down the street shouting for his mother. The butterfly left the old man's beard and flew to the mimosa tree, and a sudden gust of wind caught the torn kite and lifted it in the air, carrying it far above the struggling city into the blind blue sky.

TORIA AND THE DAUGHTER OF THE SUN

Once upon a time there was a young shepherd of the Santal tribe named Toria, who grazed his sheep and goats on the bank of a river. Now it happened that the daughters of the Sun would descend from heaven every day by means of a spider's web, to bathe in the river. Finding Toria there, they invited him to bathe with them. After they had bathed and anointed themselves with oils and perfumes, they returned to their heavenly abode, while Toria went to look after his flock.

Having become friendly with the daughters of the Sun, Toria gradually fell in love with one of them. But he was at a loss to know how to obtain such a divine creature. One day, when they met him and said, 'Come along, Toria, and bathe with us,' he suddenly thought of a plan.

While they were bathing, he said, 'Let us see who can stay under water the longest.' At a given signal, they all dived, but very soon Toria raised his head above water and, making sure that no one was looking, hurried out of the water, picked up the robe of the girl he loved and was in the act of carrying it away when the others raised their heads above the water.

The girl ran after him, begging him to return her garment, but Toria did not stop till he had reached his home. When she arrived, he gave her the robe without a word. Seeing such a beautiful and noble creature before him, for very bashfulness he could not open his mouth to ask her to marry him, so he simply said, 'You can go now.'

But she replied, 'No, I will not return. My sisters will have gone home by this time. I will stay with you and be your wife.'

All the time this was going on, a parrot, whom Toria had taught to speak, kept on flying about the heavens, calling out to the Sun: 'Oh, great Father, do not look downwards!' As a result, the Sun did not see what was happening on earth to his daughter.

This girl was very different from the women of the country—she was half-human, half-divine—so that when a beggar came to the house and saw her, his eyes were dazzled just as if he had stared at the Sun.

It happened that this same beggar, in the course of his wanderings, arrived at the king's palace, and having seen the queen, who was thought by all to be the most beautiful of women, he told the king: 'The shepherd Toria's wife is far more beautiful than your queen. If you were to see her, you would be enchanted.'

'How can I see her?' asked the king eagerly.

The beggar answered, 'Put on your old clothes and travel in disguise.'

The king did so, and having arrived at the shepherd's house, asked for alms. Toria's wife came out of the house and gave him food and water, but he was so astonished at seeing her great beauty that he was unable to eat or drink. His only thought was: How can I manage to make her my queen?

When he got home, he thought over many plans at length and decided upon one. He said, 'I will order Toria to dig a large tank with his own hands, and fill it with water, and if he does not perform the task, I will kill him and seize his wife.' He then summoned Toria to the palace, commanded him to dig the tank and threatened him with death if he failed to fill the tank with water the same night.

Toria returned home slowly and sorrowfully.

'What makes you so sad today?' asked his wife.

He replied, 'The king has ordered me to dig a large tank, to fill it with water and also to make trees grow beside it, all in the course of one night.'

'Don't let it worry you,' said his wife. 'Take your spade and mix a little water with the sand, where the tank is to be, and it will form there by itself.'

Toria did as he was told, and the king was astonished to find the tank completed in time. He had no excuse for killing Toria.

Later, the king planted a great plain with mustard seed. When it was ready for reaping, he commanded Toria to reap and gather the produce into one large heap on a certain day, failing which, he would certainly be put to death.

Toria, hearing this, was again very sad. When he told his wife about it, she said, 'Do not worry, it will be done.' So the daughter of the Sun summoned her children, the doves. They came in large numbers, and in the space of an hour, carried the produce away to the king's threshing floor. Again, Toria was saved through the wisdom of his wife. However, the king was determined not to be outdone, so he arranged a great hunt. On the day of the hunt, he assembled his retainers, and a large number of beaters and provision-carriers, and set out for the jungle. Toria was employed to carry eggs and water. But the object of the hunt was not to kill a tiger, it was to kill Toria so that the king might seize the daughter of the Sun and make her his wife.

Arriving at a cave, they said that a hare had taken refuge in it. They forced Toria into the cave. Then, rolling large stones against the entrance, they completely blocked it. They gathered large quantities of brushwood at the mouth of the cave, and set fire to it to smother Toria. Having done this, they returned home, boasting that they had finally disposed of the shepherd. But Toria broke the eggs, and all the ashes were scattered. Then he poured the water that he had with him on the remaining embers, and the fire was extinguished. Toria managed to crawl out of the cave. And there, to his great astonishment, he saw that all the white ashes of the fire were becoming cows, whilst the half-burnt wood was turning into buffaloes.

Toria herded the cows and buffaloes together, and drove them home.

When the king saw the herd, he became very envious and asked Toria where he had found such fine cows and buffaloes. Toria said, 'From that cave into which you pushed me. I did not bring many with me, being on my own. But if you and all your retainers go, you will be able to get as many as you want. But to catch them, it will be necessary to close the door of the cave and light a fire in front, as you did for me.'

'Very well,' said the king. 'I and my people will enter the cave, and, as you have sufficient cows and buffaloes, kindly do not go into the cave with us, but kindle the fire outside.'

The king and his people then entered the cave. Toria blocked up the doorway, and then lit a large fire at the entrance. Before long, all who were in the cave suffocated.

Some days later, the daughter of the Sun said, 'I want to visit my father's house.'

Toria said, 'Very well, I will also go with you.'

'No, it is foolish of you to think of such a thing,' she said.

'You will not be able to get there.'

'If you are able to go, surely I can.' And he insisted on accompanying her.

After travelling a great distance, Toria became so faint from the heat of the sun that he could go no further. His wife said, 'Did I not warn you? As for quenching your thirst, there is no water to be found here. But sit down and rest, I will see if I can find some for you.'

While she was away, driven by his great thirst, Toria sucked a raw egg that he had brought with him. No sooner had he done this than he changed into a fowl. When his wife returned with water, she could not find him anywhere; but, sitting where she had left him, was a solitary fowl. Taking the bird in her arms, she continued her journey.

When she reached her father's house, her sisters asked her, 'Where is Toria, your husband?' She replied, 'I don't know. I left him on the road while I went to fetch water. When I returned, he had disappeared. Perhaps he will turn up later.'

Her sisters, seeing the fowl, thought that it would make a good meal. And so, while Toria's wife was resting, they killed and ate the fowl. Later, when they again inquired of her as to the whereabouts of her husband, she looked thoughtful.

'I can't be sure,' she said. 'But I think you have eaten him.'

BOYHOOD DREAMS

You must pass your exams and go to college, but do not feel that if you fail, you will be able to do nothing.

My room in Shahganj was very small. I had paced about in it so often that I knew its exact measurements: twelve feet by ten. The string of my cot needed tightening. The dip in the middle was so pronounced that I invariably woke up in the morning with a backache, but I was hopeless at tightening charpoy strings.

Under the cot was my tin trunk. Its contents ranged from old, rejected manuscripts to clothes and letters and photographs. I had resolved that one day, when I had made some money with a book, I would throw the trunk and everything else out of the window, and leave Shahganj forever. But until then I was a prisoner. The rent was nominal, the window had a view of the bus stop and rickshaw stand, and I had nowhere else to go.

I did not live entirely alone. Sometimes a beggar spent the night on the balcony; and, during cold or wet weather, the boys from the tea shop, who normally slept on the pavement, crowded into the room.

Usually, I woke early in the mornings, as sleep was fitful, uneasy, crowded with dreams. I knew it was five o'clock when I heard the first upcountry bus leaving its shed. I would then get up and take a walk in the fields beyond the railroad tracks.

One morning, while I was walking in the fields, I noticed someone lying across the pathway, his head and shoulders hidden by the stalks of young sugar cane. When I came near, I saw he was a boy of about sixteen. His body was twitching convulsively, his face was very white, except where a little blood had trickled down his chin. His legs kept moving and his hands fluttered restlessly, helplessly.

'What's the matter with you?' I asked, kneeling down beside him.

But he was still unconscious and could not answer me.

I ran down the footpath to a well and, dipping the end of my shirt in a shallow trough of water, ran back and sponged the boy's face. The twitching ceased and, though he still breathed heavily, his hands became still and his face calm. He opened his eyes and stared at me without any immediate comprehension.

'You have bitten your tongue,' I said, wiping the blood from his mouth. 'Don't worry. I'll stay with you until you feel better.'

He sat up now and said, 'I'm all right, thank you.'

'What happened?' I asked, sitting down beside him.

'Oh, nothing much. It often happens, I don't know why. But I cannot control it.'

'Have you seen a doctor?'

'I went to the hospital in the beginning. They gave me some pills, which I had to take every day. But the pills made me so tired and sleepy that I couldn't work properly. So I stopped taking them. Now this happens once or twice a month. But what does it matter? I'm all right when it's over, and I don't feel anything while it is happening.'

He got to his feet, dusting his clothes and smiling at me. He was slim, long-limbed and bony. There was a little fluff on his cheeks and the promise of a moustache.

'Where do you live?' I asked. 'I'll walk back with you.'

'I don't live anywhere,' he said. 'Sometimes I sleep in the temple, sometimes in the gurdwara. In summer months, I sleep in the municipal gardens.'

'Well, then let me come with you as far as the gardens.'

He told me that his name was Kamal, that he studied at the Shahganj High School, and that he hoped to pass his examinations in a few months' time. He was studying hard and, if he passed with a good division, he hoped to attend a college. If he failed, there was only the prospect of continuing to live in the municipal gardens...

He carried with him a small tray of merchandise, supported by straps that went round his shoulders. In it were combs and buttons and cheap toys and little vials of perfume. All day, he walked about Shahganj, selling odds and ends to people in the bazaar or at their houses. He made, on an average, two rupees a day, which was enough for his food and his school fees.

He told me all this while we walked back to the bus stand. I returned to my room to try and write something, while Kamal went on to the bazaar to try and sell his wares.

There was nothing very unusual about Kamal's being an orphan and a refugee. During the communal holocaust of 1947, thousands of homes had been broken up, and women and children had been killed. What was unusual in Kamal was his sensitivity, a quality I thought rare in a Punjabi youth who had grown up in the Frontier Provinces during a period of hate and violence. And it was not so much his positive attitude to life that appealed to me (most people in Shahganj were completely resigned to their lot) as his gentleness, his quiet voice and the smile that flickered across his face regardless of whether he was sad or happy.

In the morning, when I opened my door, I found Kamal asleep at the top of the steps. His tray lay a few feet away. I shook him gently, and he woke at once.

'Have you been sleeping here all night?' I asked. 'Why didn't you come inside?'

'It was very late,' he said. 'I didn't want to disturb you.'

'Someone could have stolen your things while you slept.'

'Oh, I sleep quite lightly. Besides, I have nothing of special value. But I came to ask you something.'

'Do you need any money?'

'No. I want you to take your meal with me tonight.'

'But where? You don't have a place of your own. It will be too expensive in a restaurant.'

'In your room,' said Kamal. 'I will bring the food and cook it here. You have a stove?'

'I think so,' I said. 'I will have to look for it.'

'I will come at seven,' said Kamal, strapping on his tray. 'Don't worry. I know how to cook!'

He ran down the steps and made for the bazaar. I began to look for the oil stove, found it at the bottom of my tin trunk and then discovered I hadn't any pots or pans or dishes. Finally, I borrowed these from Deep Chand, the barber.

Kamal brought a chicken for our dinner. This was a costly luxury in Shahganj, to be taken only two or three times a year. He had bought the bird for three rupees, which was cheap, considering it was not too skinny. While Kamal set about roasting it, I went down to the bazaar and procured a bottle of beer on credit, and this served as an appetizer.

'We are having an expensive meal,' I observed. 'Three rupees for the chicken and three rupees for the beer. But I wish we could do it more often.'

'We should do it at least once a month,' said Kamal. 'It should be possible if we work hard.'

'You know how to work. You work from morning to night.'

'But you are a writer, Rusty. That is different. You have to wait for a mood.'

'Oh, I'm not a genius that I can afford the luxury of moods. No, I'm just lazy, that's all.'

'Perhaps you are writing the wrong things.'

'I know I am. But I don't know how I can write anything else.'

'Have you tried?'

'Yes, but there is no money in it. I wish I could make a living in some other way. Even if I repaired cycles, I would make more money.'

'Then why not repair cycles?'

'No, I will not repair cycles. I would rather be a bad writer than a good repairer of cycles. But let us not think of work. There is time enough for work. I want to know more about you.'

Kamal did not know if his parents were alive or dead. He had lost them, literally, when he was six. It happened at the Amritsar railroad station, where trains coming across the border disgorged thousands of refugees, or pulled into the station half-empty, drenched with blood and littered with corpses.

Kamal and his parents were lucky to escape the massacre. Had they travelled on an earlier train (they had tried desperately to get into one), they might well have been killed; but circumstances favoured them then, only to trick them later.

Kamal was clinging to his mother's sari, while she remained close to her husband, who was elbowing his way through the frightened, bewildered throng of refugees. Glancing over his shoulder at a woman who lay on the ground, wailing and beating her breasts, Kamal collided with a burly Sikh and lost his grip on his mother's sari.

The Sikh had a long curved sword at his waist, and Kamal stared up at him in awe and fascination—at his long hair, which had fallen loose, and his wild black beard and the bloodstains on his white shirt. The Sikh pushed him out of the way, and when Kamal looked around for his mother, she was not to be seen. She was hidden from him by a mass of restless bodies, pushed in different directions. He could hear her calling, 'Kamal, where are you, Kamal?' He tried to force his way through the crowd, in the direction of the voice, but he was carried the other way...

At night, when the platform was empty, he was still searching for his mother. Eventually, some soldiers took him away. They looked for his parents but without success, and finally, they sent Kamal to a refugee camp. From there, he went to an orphanage. But when he was eight and felt himself a man, he ran away.

He worked for some time as a helper in a tea shop; but, when he started getting epileptic fits, the shopkeeper asked him to leave, and he found himself on the streets, begging for a living. He begged for a year, moving from one town to another, and finally ended up at Shahganj. By then, he was twelve and too old to beg; but he had saved some money, and with it, he bought a small stock of combs, buttons, cheap perfumes and bangles; and, converting himself into a mobile shop, went from door to door, selling his wares.

Shahganj was a small town, and there was no house Kamal hadn't visited. Everyone recognized him, and there were some who offered him food and drink; the children knew him well because he played a small flute whenever he made his rounds, and they followed him to listen to the flute.

I began to look forward to Kamal's presence. He dispelled some of my own loneliness. I found I could work better, knowing that I did not have to work alone. And Kamal came to me perhaps because I was the first person to have taken a personal interest in his life, and because I saw nothing frightening in his sickness. Most people in Shahganj thought epilepsy was infectious; some considered it a form of divine punishment for sins committed in a former life. Except for children, those who knew of his condition generally gave him a wide berth.

At sixteen, a boy grows like young wheat, springing up so fast that he is unaware of what is taking place within him. His mind quickens, his gestures become more confident. Hair sprouts like young grass on his face and chest, and his muscles begin to mature. Never again will he experience so much change and growth in so short a time. He is full of currents and countercurrents.

Kamal combined the bloom of youth with the beauty of the short-lived. It made me sad even to look at his pale, slim body. It hurt me to look into his eyes. Life and death were always struggling in their depths.

'Should I go to Delhi and take up a job?' I asked.

'Why not? You are always talking about it.'

'Why don't you come too? Perhaps they can stop your fits.'

'We will need money for that. When I have passed my examinations, I will come.'

'Then I will wait,' I said. I was twenty-two, and there was world enough and time for everything.

We decided to save a little money from his small earnings and my occasional payments. We would need money to go to Delhi, money to live there until we could earn a living. We put away twenty rupees one week but lost it the next when we lent it to a friend who owned a cycle rickshaw. But this gave us the occasional use of his cycle rickshaw, and early one morning, with Kamal sitting on the crossbar, I rode out of Shahganj.

After cycling for about two miles, we got down and pushed the cycle off the road, taking a path through a paddy field and then through a field of young maize until in the distance we saw a tree, a crooked tree, growing beside an old well.

I do not know the name of that tree. I had never seen one like it before. It had a crooked trunk and crooked branches, and was clothed in thick, broad, crooked leaves, like the leaves on which food is served in the bazaar.

In the trunk of the tree there was a hole, and when we set the bicycle down with a crash, a pair of green parrots flew out, and went dipping and swerving across the fields. There was grass around the well, cropped short by grazing cattle.

We sat in the shade of the crooked tree, and Kamal untied the red cloth in which he had brought our food. When we had eaten, we stretched ourselves out on the grass. I closed my eyes and became aware of a score of different sensations. I heard a cricket singing in the tree, the cooing of pigeons from the walls of the old well, the quiet breathing of Kamal, the parrots returning to the tree, the distant hum of an aeroplane. I smelled the grass and the old bricks round the well and the promise of rain. I felt Kamal's fingers against my arm, and the sun creeping over my cheek. And when I opened my eyes, there were clouds on the horizon, and Kamal was asleep, his arm thrown across his face to keep out the glare.

I went to the well, and putting my shoulders to the ancient handle, turned the wheel, moving it around while cool, clean water gushed out over the stones and along the channel to the fields. The discovery that I could water a field, that I had the power to make things grow, gave me a thrill of satisfaction; it was like writing a story that had the ring of truth. I drank from one of the trays; the water was sweet with age.

Kamal was sitting up, looking at the sky.

'It's going to rain,' he said.

We began cycling homeward; but we were still some way out of Shahganj when it began to rain. A lashing wind swept the rain across our faces, but we exulted in it and sang at the top of our voices until we reached the Shahganj bus stop.

Across the railroad tracks and the dry riverbed, fields of maize stretched away until there came a dry region of thorn bushes and lantana scrub, where the earth was cut into jagged cracks, like a jigsaw puzzle. Dotting the landscape were old, abandoned brick kilns. When it rained heavily, the hollows filled up with water.

Kamal and I came to one of these hollows to bathe and swim. There was an island in the middle of it, and on this small mound lay the ruins of a hut where a nightwatchman had once lived, looking after the brick kilns. We would swim out to the island, which was only a few yards from the banks of the hollow. There was a grassy patch in front of the hut, and early in the mornings, before it got too hot, we would wrestle on the grass.

Though I was heavier than Kamal, my chest as sound as a new drum, he had strong, wiry arms and legs, and would often pinion me around the waist with his bony knees. Now, while we wrestled on the new monsoon grass, I felt his body go tense. He stiffened, his legs jerked against my body, and a shudder passed through him. I knew that he had a fit coming on, but I was unable to extricate myself from his arms.

He gripped me more tightly as the fit took possession of

him. Instead of struggling, I lay still, tried to absorb some of his anguish, tried to draw some of his agitation to myself. I had a strange fancy that by identifying myself with his convulsions, I might alleviate them.

I pressed against Kamal and whispered soothingly into his ear; and then, when I noticed his mouth working, I thrust my fingers between his teeth to prevent him from biting his tongue. But so violent was the convulsion that his teeth bit into the flesh of my palm and ground against my knuckles. I shouted in pain and tried to jerk my hand away, but it was impossible to loosen the grip of his jaws. So I closed my eyes and counted—counted till seven—until consciousness returned to him and his muscles relaxed.

My hand was shaking and covered with blood. I bound it in my handkerchief and kept it hidden from Kamal.

We walked back to the room without talking much. Kamal looked depressed and weak. I kept my hand beneath my shirt, and Kamal was too dejected to notice anything. It was only at night, when he returned from his classes, that he noticed the cuts, and I told him I had slipped in the road, cutting my hand on some broken glass.

Rain upon Shahganj. And, until the rain stops, Shahganj is fresh and clean and alive. The children run out of their houses, glorying in their nakedness. The gutters choke, and the narrow street becomes a torrent of water, coursing merrily down to the bus stop. It swirls over the trees and the roofs of the town, and the parched earth soaks it up, exuding a fragrance that comes only once in a year, the fragrance of quenched earth, that most exhilarating of smells.

The rain swept in through the door and soaked the cot. When I had succeeded in closing the door, I found the roof leaking, the water trickling down the walls and forming new pictures on the cracking plaster. The door flew open again, and there was Kamal standing on the threshold, shaking himself like a wet dog. Coming in, he stripped and dried himself, and then sat shivering on the bed while I made frantic efforts to close the door again.

'You need some tea,' I said.

He nodded, forgetting to smile for once, and I knew his mind was elsewhere, in one of a hundred possible places from his dreams.

'One day I will write a book,' I said as we drank strong tea in the fast-fading twilight. 'A real book, about real people. Perhaps it will be about you and me and Shahganj. And then we will run away from Shahganj, fly on the wings of Garuda and all our troubles will be over and fresh troubles will begin. Why should we mind difficulties as long as they are new difficulties?'

'First I must pass my exams,' said Kamal. 'Otherwise, I can do nothing, go nowhere.'

'Don't take exams too seriously. I know that in India they are the passport to any kind of job, and that you cannot become a clerk unless you have a degree. But do not forget that you are studying for the sake of acquiring knowledge and not for the sake of becoming a clerk. You don't want to become a clerk or a bus conductor, do you? You must pass your exams and go to college, but do not feel that if you fail, you will be able to do nothing. Why, you can start making your own buttons instead of selling other people's!'

'You are right,' said Kamal. 'But why not be an educated button manufacturer?'

'Why not, indeed? That's just what I mean. And, while you are studying for your exams, I will be writing my book.

I will start tonight! It is an auspicious night, the beginning of the monsoon.'

The light did not come on. A tree must have fallen across the wires. I lit a candle and placed it on the windowsill and, while the candle spluttered in the steamy air, Kamal opened his books and, with one hand on a book and the other hand playing with his toes—this attitude helped him to concentrate—he devoted his attention to algebra.

I took an ink bottle down from a shelf and, finding it empty, added a little rainwater to the crusted contents. Then I sat down beside Kamal and began to write; but the pen was useless and made blotches all over the paper, and I had no idea what I should write about, though I was full of writing just then. So I began to look at Kamal instead—at his eyes, hidden in shadow, and his hands, quiet in the candlelight—and I followed his breathing and the slight movement of his lips as he read softly to himself.

And, instead of starting my book, I sat and watched Kamal.

Sometimes Kamal played the flute at night while I was lying awake; and, even when I was asleep, the flute would play in my dreams. Sometimes he brought it to the crooked tree and played it for the benefit of the birds; but the parrots only made harsh noises and flew away.

Once, when Kamal was playing his flute to a group of children, he had a fit. The flute fell from his hands, and he began to roll about in the dust on the roadside. The children were frightened and ran away. But the next time they heard Kamal play his flute, they came to listen as usual.

That Kamal was gaining in strength I knew from the way he was able to pin me down whenever we wrestled on the grass near the old brick kilns. It was no longer necessary for me to yield deliberately to him. And, though his fits still recurred from time to time—as we knew they would continue to do—he was not so depressed afterwards. The anxiety and the death had gone from his eyes.

His examinations were nearing, and he was working hard. (I had yet to begin the first chapter of my book.) Because of the necessity of selling two or three rupees' worth of articles every day, he did not get much time for studying; but he stuck to his books until past midnight, and it was seldom that I heard his flute.

He put aside his tray of odds and ends during the examinations, and walked to the examination centre instead. And after two weeks, when it was all over, he took up his tray and began his rounds again. In a burst of creativity, I wrote three pages of my novel.

On the morning the results of the examination were due, I rose early, before Kamal, and went down to the news agency. It was five o'clock, and the newspapers had just arrived. I went through the columns relating to Shahganj, but I couldn't find Kamal's roll number on the list of successful candidates. I had the number written down on a slip of paper, and I looked at it again to make sure that I had compared it correctly with the others; then I went through the newspaper once more.

When I returned to the room, Kamal was sitting on the doorstep. I didn't have to tell him he had failed. He knew by the look on my face. I sat down beside him, and we said nothing for some time.

'Never mind,' said Kamal, eventually. 'I will pass next year.'

I realized that I was more depressed than he was, and that he was trying to console me.

'If only you'd had more time,' I said.

'I have plenty of time now. Another year. And you will

have time in which to finish your book; then we can both go away. Another year of Shahganj won't be so bad. As long as I have your friendship, almost everything else can be tolerated, even my sickness.'

And then, turning to me with an expression of intense happiness, he said, 'Yesterday I was sad, and tomorrow I may be sad again, but today I know that I am happy. I want to live on and on. I feel that life isn't long enough to satisfy me.'

He stood up, the tray hanging from his shoulders.

'What would you like to buy?' he said. 'I have everything you need.'

At the bottom of the steps, he turned and smiled at me, and I knew then that I had written my story.

CHILDREN OF INDIA

They pass me every day, on their way to school—boys and girls from the surrounding villages and the outskirts of the hill station. There are no school buses plying for these children, they walk.

For many of them, it's a very long walk to school.

Ranbir, who is ten, has to climb the mountain from his village, four miles away and 2,000 feet below the town level. He comes in all weathers, wearing the same pair of cheap shoes until they have almost fallen apart.

Ranbir is a cheerful soul. He waves to me whenever he sees me at my window. Sometimes he brings me cucumbers from his father's field. I pay him for the cucumbers; he uses the money for books or for small things needed at home.

Many of the children are like Ranbir—poor but slightly better off than what their parents were at the same age. They cannot attend the expensive residential and private schools that abound here but must go to the government-aided schools with only basic facilities. Not many of their parents managed to go to school. They spent their lives working in the fields or delivering milk in the hill station. The lucky ones got into the army. Perhaps Ranbir will do something different when he grows up.

He has yet to see a train, but he sees planes flying over the mountains almost every day.

'How far can a plane go?' he asks.

'All over the world,' I tell him. 'Thousands of miles in a day. You can go almost anywhere.'

'I'll go round the world one day,' he vows. 'I'll buy a plane and go everywhere!'

And maybe he will. He has a determined chin and a defiant look in his eye.

The following lines in my journal were put down for my own inspiration or encouragement, but they will do for any determined young person:

> We get out of life what we bring to it. There is not a dream that may not come true if we have the energy that determines our own fate. We can always get what we want if we will it intensely enough...So few people succeed greatly because so few people conceive a great end, working towards it without giving up. We all know that the man who works steadily for money gets rich; the man who works day and night for fame or power reaches his goal. And those who work for deeper, more spiritual achievements will find them too. It may come when we no longer have any use for it, but if we have been willing it long enough, it will come!

◆

Up to a few years ago, very few girls in the hills or in the villages of India went to school. They helped in the home until they were old enough to be married, which wasn't very old. But there are now just as many girls as there are boys going to school.

Bindra is something of an extrovert—a confident fourteen-year-old who chatters away as she hurries down the road with her companions. Her father is a forest guard and knows me quite well: I meet him on my walks through the deodar woods behind Landour. And I had grown used to seeing Bindra almost every day. When she did not put in an appearance for a week, I asked her brother if anything was wrong.

'Oh, nothing,' he says, 'she is helping my mother cut grass. Soon the monsoon will end and the grass will dry up. So we cut it now and store it for the cows for winter.'

'And why aren't you cutting grass too?'

'Oh, I have a cricket match today,' he says and hurries away to join his team-mates. Unlike his sister, he puts pleasure before work!

Cricket, once the game of the elite, has become the game of the masses. On any holiday, in any part of this vast country, groups of boys can be seen making their way to the nearest field, or open patch of land, with bat, ball and any other cricketing gear that they can cobble together. Watching some of them play, I am amazed at the quality of talent, at the finesse with which they bat or bowl. Some of the local teams are as good, if not better, than any from the private schools, where there are better facilities. But the boys from these poor or lower-middle-class families will never get the exposure that is necessary to bring them to the attention of those who select state or national teams. They will never get near enough to the men of influence and power. They must continue to play for the love of the game, or watch their more fortunate heroes' exploits on television.

■

As winter approaches and the days grow shorter, those children who live far away must quicken their pace in order to get home before dark. Ranbir and his friends find that darkness has fallen before they are halfway home.

'What is the time, Uncle?' he asks as he trudges up the steep road past Ivy Cottage.

One gets used to being called 'Uncle' by almost every boy or girl one meets. I wonder how the custom began. Perhaps it has its origins in the folk tale about the tiger who refrained from pouncing on you if you called him 'Uncle'. Tigers don't eat their relatives! Or do they? The ploy may not work if the tiger happens to be a tigress. Would you call her 'Aunty' as she (or your teacher!) descends on you?

It's dark at six, and by then, Ranbir likes to be out of the deodar forest and on the open road to the village. The moon and the stars and the village lights are sufficient, but not in the forest, where it is dark even during the day. And the silent flitting of bats and flying foxes, and the eerie hoot of an owl can be a little disconcerting for the hardiest of children. Once Ranbir and the other boys were chased by a bear.

When he told me about it, I said, 'Well, now we know you can run faster then a bear!'

'Yes, but you have to run downhill when chased by a bear.' He spoke as one having long experience of escaping from bears. 'They run much faster uphill!'

'I'll remember that,' I said, 'Thanks for the advice.' And I don't suppose calling a bear 'Uncle' would help.

Usually, Ranbir has the company of other boys, and they sing most of the way, for loud singing by small boys will silence owls and frighten away the forest demons. One of them plays a flute, and flute music in the mountains is always enchanting.

∎

Not only in the hills but all over India, children are constantly making their way to and from school, in conditions that range from dust storms in the Rajasthan desert to blizzards in Ladakh and Kashmir. In the larger towns and cities, there are school buses, but in remote rural areas, getting to school can pose a problem.

Most children are more than equal to any obstacles that may arise. Like those youngsters in the Ganjam district of Orissa, in the absence of a bridge, they swim or wade across the Dhanei River every day in order to reach their school. I have a picture of them in my scrapbook. Holding books or satchels aloft in one hand, they do the breast stroke or dog-paddle with the other, or form a chain and help each other across.

Wherever you go in India, you will find children helping out with the family's source of livelihood, whether it be drying fish on the Malabar coast or gathering saffron buds in Kashmir or grazing camels or cattle in a village in Rajasthan or Gujarat.

Only the more fortunate can afford to send their children to English-medium private or 'public' schools, and those children really are fortunate, for some of these institutions are excellent schools, as good, and often better, than their counterparts in Britain or the US. Whether it's in Ajmer or Bangalore, New Delhi or Chandigarh, Kanpur or Calcutta, the best schools set very high standards. The growth of a prosperous middle class has led to an ever-increasing demand for quality education. But as private schools proliferate, standards suffer too, and many parents must settle for the second-rate.

The great majority of our children still attend schools run by the state or municipality. These vary from the good to the bad to the ugly, depending on how they are run and where they are situated. A classroom without windows or with a roof that lets in the monsoon rain is not uncommon. Even so, children from different communities learn to live and grow together. Hardship makes brothers of us all.

The census tells us that two in every five of the population is in the age group of five to fifteen. Almost half our population is on the way to school!

And here I stand at my window, watching some of them pass by—boys and girls, big and small, some scruffy, some smart, some mischievous, some serious, but all *going* somewhere—hopefully towards a better future.

UP THE SPIRAL STAIRCASE

We lived in an old palace beside a lake. The palace looked a ruin from the outside, but the rooms were cool and comfortable. We lived in one wing, and my father organized a small school in another wing. His pupils were the children of the raja and the raja's relatives. My father had started life in India as a tea planter; but he had been trained as a teacher, and the idea of starting a school in a small state facing the Arabian Sea had appealed to him. The pay wasn't much, but we had a palace to live in, the latest 1938 model Hillman to drive about in, and a number of servants. In those days, of course, everyone had servants (although the servants did not have any). Ayah was our own; but the cook, the bearer, the gardener and the bhisti were all provided by the state.

Sometimes, I sat in the schoolroom with the other children (who were all much bigger than me), sometimes I remained in the house with Ayah, sometimes I followed the gardener Dukhi about the spacious garden.

Dukhi means 'sad', and though I never could discover if the gardener had anything to feel sad about, the name certainly suited him. He had grown to resemble the drooping weeds that he was always digging up with a tiny spade. I seldom saw him standing up. He always sat on the ground with his knees well up to his chin, and attacked the weeds from this position. He could spend all day on his haunches, moving about the garden simply by shuffling his feet along the grass.

I tried to imitate his posture, sitting down on my heels and putting my knees into my armpits, but could never hold the position for more than five minutes.

Time had no meaning in a large garden, and Dukhi never hurried. Life, for him, was not a matter of one year succeeding another but of five seasons—winter, spring, hot weather, monsoon and autumn—arriving and departing. His seedbeds had to always be in readiness for the coming season, and he did not look any further than the next monsoon. It was impossible to tell his age. He may have been thirty-six or eighty-six. He was either very young for his years or very old for them.

Dukhi loved bright colours, especially reds and yellows. He liked strongly scented flowers, like jasmine and honeysuckle. He couldn't understand my father's preference for the more delicately perfumed petunias and sweet peas. But I shared Dukhi's fondness for the common, bright orange marigold, which is offered in temples and used to make garlands and nosegays. When the garden was bare of all colour, the marigold would still be there, gay and flashy, challenging the sun.

Dukhi was very fond of making nosegays, and I liked to watch him at work. A sunflower formed the centrepiece. It was surrounded by roses, marigolds and oleanders, fringed with green leaves, and bound together with silver thread. The perfume was overpowering. The nosegays were presented to me or my father on special occasions, that is, on birthdays or any party, at moments of arrival or departure, or to guests of my father's who were considered important.

One day I found Dukhi making a nosegay, and said, 'No one is coming today, Dukhi. It isn't even a birthday.'

'It is a birthday, chota sahib,' he said. 'Chota sahib' was the title he had given me. It wasn't much of a title compared to raja sahib or diwan sahib or burra sahib but it was nice to have a title at the age of seven.

'Oh,' I said. 'And is there a party, too?'

'No party.'

'What's the use of a birthday without a party? What's the use of a party without presents?'

'This person doesn't like presents—just flowers.'

'Who is it?' I asked, full of curiosity.

'If you want to find out, you can take these flowers to her. She lives right at the top of the far side of the palace. There are twenty-two steps to climb. Remember that, chota sahib. If you take twenty-three steps, you will go over the edge into the lake!'

◆

I started climbing the stairs.

It was a spiral staircase of wrought iron, and it went round and round and up and up, and it made me quite dizzy and tired.

At the top, I found myself on a small balcony which looked out, over the lake and another palace, at the crowded town and the distant harbour. I heard a voice, a rather high, musical voice saying (in English), 'Are you a ghost?' I turned to see who had spoken but found the balcony empty. The voice had come from a dark room.

I turned to the stairway, ready to flee, but the voice said, 'Oh, don't go, there's nothing to be frightened of!'

And so I stood still, peering cautiously into the darkness of the room.

'First tell me—are you a ghost?'

'I'm a boy,' I said.

'And I'm a girl. We can be friends. I can't come out there, so you had better come in. Come along, I'm not a ghost either—not yet, anyway!'

As there was nothing very frightening about the voice, I stepped into the room. It was dark inside, and, coming in from the glare, it took me some time to make out the tiny, elderly lady seated on a cushioned, gilt chair. She wore a red sari, lots of coloured bangles on her wrists, and golden earrings. Her hair was streaked with white, but her skin was still quite smooth and unlined, and she had large and very beautiful eyes.

'You must be Master Bond!' she said. 'Do you know who I am?'

'You're a lady with a birthday,' I said, 'but that's all I know. Dukhi didn't tell me anymore.'

'If you promise to keep it a secret, I'll tell you who I am. You see, everyone thinks I am mad. Do you think so, too?'

'I don't know.'

'Well, you must tell me if you think so,' she said with a chuckle. Her laugh was the sort of sound made by the gecko, coming from deep in the throat. 'I have a feeling you are a truthful boy. Do you find it very difficult to tell the truth?'

'Sometimes.'

'Sometimes. Of course, there are times when I tell lies—lots of little lies—because they're such fun! But would you call me a liar? I wouldn't, if I were you, but *would* you?'

'Are you a liar?'

'I'm asking you! If I were to tell you that I was a queen—that I am a queen—would you believe me?'

I thought deeply about this, and then said, 'I'll try to believe you.'

'Oh, but you *must* believe me. I am a real queen, I'm a

rani. Look I've got diamonds to prove it.' And she held out her hands, and there was a ring on each finger, the stones glowing and glittering in the dim light. 'Diamonds, rubies, pearls and emeralds! Only a queen can have these!' She was most anxious that I should believe her.

'You must be a queen,' I said.

'Right!' she snapped. 'In that case, would you mind calling me "Your Highness"?'

'Your Highness,' I said.

She smiled. It was a slow, beautiful smile. All her face lit up.

'I could love you,' she said. 'But better still, I'll give you something to eat. Do you like chocolates?'

'Yes, Your Highness.'

'Well,' she said, taking a box from the table beside her, 'these have come all the way from England. Take two. Only two, mind you, otherwise the box will finish before Saturday, and I don't want that to happen because I won't get any more till Saturday. That's when Captain MacWhirr's ship sets in, the *SS Lucy* loaded with boxes and boxes of chocolates!'

'All for you?' I asked in considerable awe.

'Yes, of course. They have to last at least three months. I get them from England. I get only the best chocolates. I like them with pink, crunchy fillings, don't you?'

'Oh, yes!' I exclaimed, full of envy.

'Never mind,' she said. 'I may give you one now and then—if you're very nice to me. Here you are, help yourself...' She pushed the chocolate box towards me.

I took a silver-wrapped chocolate, and then just as I was thinking of taking a second one, she quickly took the box away.

'No more!' she said, 'They have to last till Saturday.'

'But I took only one,' I said with some indignation.

'Did you?' She gave me a sharp look, decided I was telling the truth, and said graciously, 'Well, in that case you can have another.'

Watching the rani carefully, in case she snatched the box away again, I selected a second chocolate, this one with a green wrapper. I don't remember what kind of a day it was outside, but I remember the bright green of the chocolate wrapper.

I thought it would be rude to eat the chocolates in front of a queen, so I put them in my pocket and said, 'I'd better go now. Ayah will be looking for me.'

'And when will you be coming to see me again?'

'I don't know,' I said.

'Your Highness.'

'Your Highness.'

'There's something I want you to do for me,' she said, placing one little finger on my shoulder and giving me a conspiratorial look. 'Will you do it?'

'What is it, Your Highness?'

'What is it? Why do you ask? A real prince never asks where or why or whatever, he simply does what the princess asks of him. When I was a princess—before I became a queen, that is—I asked a prince to swim across the lake and fetch me a lily growing on the other bank.'

'And did he get it for you?'

'He drowned halfway across. Let that be a lesson to you. Never agree to do something without knowing what it is.'

'But I thought you said...'

'Never mind what I *said*. It's what I *say* that matters!'

'Oh, all right,' I said, fidgeting to be gone. 'What is it you want me to do?'

'Nothing.' Her tiny rosebud lips pouted and she stared

sullenly at a picture on the wall. Now that my eyes had grown used to the dim light in the room, I noticed that the walls were filled with portraits of stout rajas and ranis, turbaned and bedecked in fine clothes. There were also portraits of Queen Victoria and King George V of England. And, in the centre of all this distinguished company, a large picture of Mickey Mouse.

'I'll do it if it isn't too dangerous,' I said.

'Then, listen.' She took my hand and drew me towards her—what a tiny hand she had!—and whispered, 'I want a red rose. From the palace garden. But be careful! Don't let Dukhi the gardener catch you. He'll know it's for me. He knows I love roses. And he hates me! I'll tell you why, one day. But if he catches you, he'll do something terrible.'

'To me?'

'No, to himself. That's much worse, isn't it? He'll tie himself into knots, or lie naked on a bed of thorns, or go on a long fast with nothing to eat but fruit, sweets and chicken! So you will be careful, won't you?'

'Oh, but he doesn't hate you,' I cried in protest, remembering the flowers he'd sent for her, and looking around, I found that I'd been sitting on them. 'Look, he sent these flowers for your birthday!'

'Well, if he sent them for my birthday, you can take them back,' she snapped. 'But if he sent them for me...' and she suddenly softened and looked coy, 'then I might keep them. Thank you, my dear, it was a very sweet thought.' And she leant forwards as though to kiss me.

'It's late, I must go!' I said in alarm, and turning on my heels, ran out of the room and down the spiral staircase.

BUS STOP, PIPALNAGAR

I

My balcony was my window to the world.

The room itself had only one window, a square hole in the wall crossed by two iron bars. The view from it was rather restricted. If I craned my neck sideways and put my nose to the bars, I could see the end of the building. Below was a narrow courtyard where children played. Across the courtyard, on level with my room, were three separate windows belonging to three separate rooms, each window barred in the same way, with iron bars. During the day, it was difficult to see into these rooms. The harsh, cruel sunlight filled the courtyard, making the windows patches of darkness.

My room was very small. I had paced about in it so often that I knew its exact measurements. My foot, from heel to toe, was eleven inches long. That made my room just over fifteen feet in length; for, when I measured the last foot, my toes turned up against the wall. It wasn't more than eight feet broad, which meant that two people was the most it could comfortably accommodate. I was the only tenant, but at times, I had put up at least three friends—two on the floor, two on the bed. The plaster had been peeling off the walls, and in addition, the greasy stains and patches were difficult to hide, though I covered the worst ones with pictures cut out from magazines—Waheeda Rehman, the Indian actress, successfully blotted out one big patch and a recent Mr Universe displayed his muscles from the opposite wall. The biggest stain was all but concealed by a calendar that showed Ganesh, the elephant-headed god, whose blessings were vital to all good beginnings.

My belongings were few. A shelf on the wall supported an untidy pile of paperbacks, and a small table in one corner of the room supported the solid weight of my rejected manuscripts and an ancient typewriter which I had obtained on hire.

I was eighteen years old and a writer.

Such a combination would be disastrous enough anywhere, but in India, it was doubly so; for there were not many papers to write for and payments were small. In addition, I was very inexperienced and though what I wrote came from the heart, only a fraction touched the hearts of editors. Nevertheless, I persevered and was able to earn about a hundred rupees a month, barely enough to keep body, soul and typewriter together. There wasn't much else I could do. Without that passport to a job—a university degree—I had no alternative but to accept the classification of 'self-employed'—which was impressive as it included doctors, lawyers, property dealers and grain merchants, most of whom earned well over a thousand rupees a month.

'Haven't you realized that India is bursting with young people trying to pass exams?' asked a journalist friend. 'It's a desperate matter, this race for academic qualifications. Everyone wants to pass his exam the easy way, without reading too many books or attending more than half-a-dozen lectures. That's where a smart fellow like you comes in! Why would students wade through five volumes of political history when they can buy a few model answer papers at any bookstall? They are helpful, these guess papers. You can write them quickly and flood the market. They'll sell like hot cakes!'

'Who eats hot cakes here?'

'Well, then, hot chapattis.'

'I'll think about it,' I said; but the idea repelled me. If I was going to misguide students, I would rather do it by writing second-rate detective stories than by providing them with ready-made answer papers. Besides, I thought it would bore me.

II

The string of the cot needed tightening. The dip in the middle of the bed was so bad that I woke up in the morning with a stiff back. But I was hopeless at tightening bed strings and would have to wait until one of the boys from the tea shop paid me a visit. I was too tall for the cot, anyway, and if my feet didn't stick out at one end, my head lolled over the other.

Under the cot was my tin trunk. Apart from my clothes, it contained notebooks, diaries, photographs, scrapbooks and other odds and ends that form a part of a writer's existence.

I did not live entirely alone. During cold or rainy weather, the boys from the tea shop, who normally slept on the pavement, crowded into the room. Apart from them, there were lizards on the walls and ceilings—friends these—and a large rat—definitely an enemy—who got in and out of the window, and who sometimes carried away manuscripts and clothing.

June nights were the most uncomfortable. Mosquitoes emerged from all the ditches, gullies and ponds, to swarm over Pipalnagar. Bugs, finding it uncomfortable inside the woodwork of the cot, scrambled out at night and found their way under the sheet. The lizards wandered listlessly over the walls, impatient for the monsoon rains, when they would be able to feast on thousands of insects.

Everyone in Pipalnagar was waiting for the cool, quenching relief of the monsoon.

III

I woke every morning at five as soon as the first bus moved out of the shed, situated only twenty or thirty yards down the road. I dressed, went down to the tea shop for a glass of hot tea and some buttered toast, and then visited Deep Chand the barber at his shop.

At eighteen, I shaved about three times a week. Sometimes, I shaved myself. But often, when I felt lazy, Deep Chand shaved me, at the special concessional rate of two annas.

'Give my head a good massage, Deep Chand,' I said. 'My brain is not functioning these days. In my latest story, there are three murders, but it is boring just the same.'

'You must write a good book,' said Deep Chand, beginning the ritual of the head massage, his fingers squeezing my temples and tugging at my hair-roots. 'Then you can make some money and clear out of Pipalnagar. Delhi is the place to go! Why, I know a man who arrived in Delhi in 1947 with nothing but the clothes he wore and a few rupees. He began by selling thirsty travellers glasses of cold water at the railway station, then he opened a small tea shop; now he has two big restaurants and lives in a house as large as the prime minister's!'

Nobody intended to live in Pipalnagar forever. Delhi was the city most aspired to, but as it was 200 miles away, few could afford to travel there.

Deep Chand would have shifted his trade to another town

if he had had the capital. In Pipalnagar, his main customers were small shopkeepers, factory workers and labourers from the railway station. 'Here, I can charge only six annas for a haircut,' he lamented. 'In Delhi, I could charge a rupee.'

IV

I was walking in the wheat fields beyond the railway tracks when I noticed a boy lying across the footpath, his head and shoulders hidden by wheat plants. I walked faster, and when I came near, I saw that the boy's legs were twitching. He seemed to be having some kind of fit. The boy's face was white, his legs kept moving and his hands fluttered restlessly among the wheat stalks.

'What's the matter?' I said, kneeling down beside him, but he was still unconscious.

I ran down the path to a Persian well, and dipping the end of my shirt in a shallow trough of water, soaked it well before returning to the boy. As I sponged his face the twitching ceased, and though he still breathed heavily, his face was calm and his hands still. He opened his eyes and stared at me, but he didn't really see me.

'You have bitten your tongue,' I said, wiping a little blood from the corner of his mouth. 'Don't worry. I'll stay here with you until you are all right.'

The boy raised himself and, resting his chin on his knees, he passed his arms around his drawn-up legs.

'I'm all right now,' he said.

'What happened?' I asked, sitting down beside him.

'Oh, it is nothing, it often happens. I don't know why. I cannot control it.'

'Have you been to a doctor?'

'Yes, when the fits first started, I went to the hospital. They gave me some pills that I had to take every day. But the pills made me so tired and sleepy that I couldn't work properly. So I stopped taking them. Now this happens once or twice a week. What does it matter? I'm all right when it's over and I do not feel anything when it happens.'

He got to his feet, dusting his clothes and smiling at me. He was a slim boy, long-limbed and bony. There was a little fluff on his cheeks and the promise of a moustache. He told me his name was Suraj, that he went to a night school in the city, and that he hoped to finish his high school exams in a few months' time. He was studying hard, he said, and if he passed, he hoped to get a scholarship to a good college. If he failed, there was only the prospect of continuing in Pipalnagar.

I noticed a small tray of merchandise lying on the ground. It contained combs and buttons and little bottles of perfume. The tray was made to hang at Suraj's waist, supported by straps that went around his shoulders. All day he walked about Pipalnagar, sometimes covering ten or fifteen miles, selling odds and ends to people in their houses. He averaged about two rupees a day, which was enough for his food and other necessities; he managed to save about ten rupees a month for his school fees. He ate irregularly at little tea shops, at the stall near the bus stop, under the shady jamun and mango trees. When the jamun fruit was ripe, he would sit on a tree, sucking the sour fruit until his lips were stained purple. There was a small, nagging fear that he might get a fit while sitting on the tree and fall off, but the temptation to eat jamun was greater than his fear.

All this he told me while we walked through the fields towards the bazaar.

'Where do you live?' I asked. 'I'll walk home with you.'

'I don't live anywhere,' said Suraj. 'My home is not in Pipalnagar. Sometimes, I sleep at the temple or at the railway station. In the summer months, I sleep on the grass of the municipal park.'

'Well, wherever it is you stay, let me come with you.'

We walked together into the town, and parted near the bus stop. I returned to my room, and tried to do some writing while Suraj went to the bazaar to try selling his wares. We had agreed to meet each other again. I realized that Suraj was an epileptic, but there was nothing unusual about him being an orphan and a refugee. I liked his positive attitude to life. Most people in Pipalnagar were resigned to their circumstances, but he was ambitious. I also liked his gentleness, his quiet voice, and the smile that flickered across his face regardless of whether he was sad or happy.

V

The temperature had touched forty-three degrees Celsius, and the small streets of Pipalnagar were empty. To walk barefoot on the scorching pavements was possible only for labourers, whose feet had developed several hard layers of protective skin; and now even these hardy men lay stretched out in the shade provided by trees and buildings.

I hadn't written anything in two weeks, and though one or two small payments were due from a Delhi newspaper, I could think of no substantial amount that was likely to come my way in the near future. I decided that I would dash off a couple of articles that same night and post them the following morning.

Having made this comforting decision, I lay down on the

floor in preference to the cot. I liked the touch of things; the touch of a cool floor on a hot day, the touch of earth—soft, grassy grass was good, especially dew-drenched grass. Wet earth was soft, sensuous, as was splashing through puddles and streams.

I slept, and dreamt of a cool, clear stream in a forest glade, where I bathed in gay abandon. A little further downstream was another bather. I hailed him, expecting to see Suraj but when the bather turned I found that it was my landlord's pot-bellied rent collector, holding an accounts ledger in his hands. This woke me up, and for the remainder of the day I worked feverishly at my articles.

Next morning, when I opened the door, I found Suraj asleep at the top of the steps. His tray lay at the bottom of the steps. He woke up as soon as I touched his shoulder.

'Have you been sleeping here all night?' I asked. 'Why didn't you come in?'

'It was very late,' said Suraj. 'I didn't want to disturb you.'

'Someone could have stolen your things while you were asleep.'

'Oh, I sleep quite lightly. Besides, I have nothing of great value. But I came here to ask you a favour.'

'You need money?'

He laughed. 'Do all your friends mean money when they ask for favours? No, I want you to take your meal with me tonight.'

'But where? You have no place of your own and it would be too expensive in a restaurant.'

'In your room,' said Suraj. 'I shall bring the meat and vegetables and cook them here. Do you have a cooker?'

'I think so,' I said, scratching my head in some perplexity. 'I will have to look for it.'

Suraj brought a chicken for dinner—a luxury, one to be indulged in only two or three times a year. He had bought the bird for seven rupees, which was cheap. We spiced it and roasted it on a spit.

'I wish we could do this more often,' I said, as I dug my teeth into the soft flesh of a second chicken leg.

'We could do it at least once a month if we worked hard,' said Suraj.

'You know how to work. You work from morning to evening and then you work again.'

'But you are a writer. That is different. You have to wait for the right moment.'

I laughed. 'Moods and moments are for geniuses. No, it's really a matter of working hard, and I'm just plain lazy, to tell you the truth.'

'Perhaps you are writing the wrong things.'

'Perhaps, I wish I could do something else. Even if I repaired bicycle tyres, I'd make more money!'

'Then why don't you repair bicycle tyres?'

'Oh, I would rather be a bad writer than a good repairer of cycle tyres.' I brightened up, 'I could go into business, though. Do you know I once owned a vegetable stall?'

'Wonderful! When was that?'

'A couple of months ago. But it failed after two days.'

'Then you are not good at business. Let us think of something else.'

'I can tell fortunes with cards.'

'There are already too many fortune tellers in Pipalnagar.'

'Then we won't talk of fortunes. And you must sleep here tonight. It is better than sleeping on the roadside.'

VI

At noon when the shadows shifted and crossed the road, a band of children rushed down the empty street, shouting and waving their satchels. They had been at their desks from early morning, and now, despite the hot sun, they would have their fling while their elders slept on string charpoys beneath leafy neem trees.

On the soft sand near the riverbed, boys wrestled or played leapfrog. At alley corners, where tall buildings shaded narrow passages, the favourite game was gulli-danda. The gulli—a small piece of wood, about four inches long sharpened to a point at each end—is struck with the danda—a short, stout stick. A player is allowed three hits, and his score is the distance, in danda lengths, of his hits of the gulli. Boys who were experts at the game sent the gulli flying far down the road—sometimes into a shop or through a windowpane, which resulted in confusion, loud invective, and a dash for cover.

A game for both children and young men was kabaddi. This is a game that calls for good breath control and much agility. It is also known in different parts of India as hootoo-too, kho-kho and atya patya. Ramu, Deep Chand's younger brother, excelled at this game. He was the Pipalnagar kabaddi champion.

The game is played by two teams, consisting of eight or nine members each, who face each other across a dividing line. Each side, in turn, sends out one of its players into the opponent's area. This person has to keep on saying 'kabaddi, kabaddi' very fast and without taking a second breath. If he returns to his side after touching an opponent, that opponent is 'dead' and out of the game. If, however, he is caught and cannot struggle back to his side while still holding his breath, he is 'dead'.

Ramu, who was also a good wrestler, knew all the kabaddi

holds, and was particularly good at capturing opponents. He had vitality and confidence, rare things in Pipalnagar. He wanted to go into the army after finishing school, a happy choice I thought.

VII

Suraj did not know if his parents were dead or alive. He had literally lost them when he was six. His father had been a farmer, a dark, unfathomable man who spoke little, thought perhaps even less and was vaguely aware he had a son—a weak boy given to introspection and dawdling at the riverbank when he should have been helping in the fields.

Suraj's mother had been a subdued, silent woman, frail and consumptive. Her husband seemed to expect that she would not live long, but Suraj did not know if she was living or dead. He had lost his parents at Amritsar railway station in the days of Partition, when trains coming across the border from Pakistan disgorged themselves of thousands of refugees or pulled into the station half-empty, drenched with blood and littered with corpses.

Suraj and his parents had been lucky to escape one of these massacres. Had they travelled on an earlier train (which they had tried desperately to catch), they might have been killed. Suraj was clinging to his mother's sari while she tried to keep up with her husband who was elbowing his way through the frightened, bewildered throng of refugees. Suraj collided with a burly Sikh and lost his grip on the sari. The Sikh had a long curved sword at his waist, and Suraj stared up at him in awe and fascination—at the man's long hair, which had fallen loose, at his wild black beard, and at the bloodstains on his white shirt. The Sikh pushed him aside and when Suraj looked around for his mother, she was not to be seen. She was hidden from him by a mass of restless bodies, all pushing in different directions. He could hear her calling his name and he tried to force his way through the crowd in the direction of her voice, but he was carried on the other way.

At night, when the platform emptied, he was still searching for his mother. Eventually, the police came and took him away. They looked for his parents but without success, and finally they sent him to a home for orphans. Many children lost their parents at about the same time.

Suraj stayed at the orphanage for two years and when he was eight, and felt himself a man, he ran away. He worked for some time as a helper in a tea shop; but when he started having epileptic fits, the shopkeeper asked him to leave, and the boy found himself on the streets, begging for a living. He begged for a year, moving from one town to the next and finally ended up in Pipalnagar. By then, he was twelve and really too old to beg, but he had saved some money, and with it he bought a small stock of combs, buttons, cheap perfumes and bangles, and, converting himself into a mobile shop, went from door to door selling his wares.

Pipalnagar is a small town and there was no house which Suraj hadn't visited. Everyone knew him; some had offered him food and drinks; and the children liked him because he often played on a small flute when he went on his rounds.

VIII

Suraj came to see me quite often and, when he stayed late, he slept in my room, curling up on the floor and sleeping fitfully. He would always leave early in the morning before I could get him anything to eat.

'Should I go to Delhi, Suraj?' I asked him one evening.

'Why not? In Delhi, there are many ways of making money.'

'And spending it too. Why don't you come with me?'

'After my exams, perhaps. Not now.'

'Well, I can wait. I don't want to live alone in a big city.'

'In the meantime, write your book.'

'All right, I will try.'

We decided we could try to save a little money from Suraj's earnings and my own occasional payments from newspapers and magazines. Even if we were to give Delhi only a few days' trial, we would need money to live on. We managed to put away twenty rupees one week, but withdrew it the next when a friend, Pitamber, asked for a loan to repair his cycle rickshaw. He returned the money in three instalments but we could not save any of it. Pitamber and Deep Chand also had plans of going to Delhi. Pitamber wanted to own his own cycle rickshaw; Deep Chand dreamt of a swanky barber shop in the capital.

One day Suraj and I hired bicycles and rode out of Pipalnagar. It was a hot, sunny morning and we were perspiring after we had gone two miles, but a fresh wind sprang up suddenly, and we could smell the rain in the air though there were no clouds to be seen.

'Let us go where there are no people at all,' said Suraj. 'I am a little tired of people. I see too many of them all day.'

We got down from our cycles and, pushing them off the road, took a path through a paddy field and then one through a field of young maize, and in the distance we saw a tree, a crooked tree, growing beside a well. Even today, I do not know the name of that tree. I had never seen its kind before. It had a crooked trunk, crooked branches and it was clothed in thick, broad, crooked leaves, like the leaves on which food is served in bazaars.

In the trunk of the tree was a large hole and when I sat my cycle down with a crash, two green parrots flew out of the hole, and went dipping and swerving across the fields.

There was grass around the well, cropped short by grazing cattle, so we sat in the shade of the crooked tree and Suraj untied the red cloth in which we had brought food. We ate our bread and vegetable curry; meanwhile the parrots returned to the tree.

'Let us come here every week,' said Suraj, stretching himself out on the grass. It was a drowsy day, the air was humid and he soon fell asleep. I was aware of different sensations. I heard a cricket singing in the tree; the cooing of pigeons which lived in the walls of the old well; the soft breathing of Suraj; a rustling in the leaves of the tree; the distant drone of the bees. I smelt the grass and the old bricks around the well, and the promise of rain.

When I opened my eyes, I saw dark clouds on the horizon. Suraj was still sleeping with his arms thrown across his face to keep the glare out of his eyes. As I was thirsty, I went to the well and, putting my shoulders to it, turned the wheel very slowly, walking around the well four times, while cool clean water gushed out over the stones and along the channel to the fields. I drank from one of the trays, and the water tasted sweet; the deeper the wells, the sweeter the water. Suraj was sitting up now, looking at the sky.

'It's going to rain,' he said.

We pushed our cycles back to the main road and began riding homewards. We were a mile out of Pipalnagar when it began to rain. A lashing wind swept the rain across our faces, but we exulted in it and sang at the top of our voices until we reached the bus stop. Leaving the cycles at the hire shop, we ran up the rickety, swaying steps to my room.

In the evening, as the bazaar was lighting up, the rain stopped. We went to sleep quite early, but at midnight I was woken by the moon shining full on my face—a full moon, shedding its light all over Pipalnagar, peeping and prying into every home, washing the empty streets, silvering the corrugated tin roofs.

IX

The lizards hung listlessly on the walls and ceilings, waiting for the monsoon rains, which bring out all the insects from their cracks and crannies.

One day, clouds loomed upon the horizon, growing rapidly into enormous towers. A faint breeze sprang up, bringing with it the first of the monsoon raindrops. This was the moment everyone was waiting for. People ran out of their houses to take in the fresh breeze and the scent of those first few raindrops on the parched, dusty earth. Underground, in their cracks, the insects were moving. Termites and white ants, which had been sleeping through the hot season, emerged from their lairs.

And then, on the second or third night of the monsoon, came the great yearly flight of insects into the cool, brief freedom of the night. Out of every crack, from under the roots of trees, huge winged ants emerged, at first fluttering about heavily, on the first and last flight of their lives. At night, there was only one direction in which they could fly—towards the light; towards the electric bulbs and smoky kerosene lamps throughout Pipalnagar. The street lamp opposite the bus stop, beneath my room, attracted a massive, quivering swarm of clumsy termites, which gave the impression of one thick, slowly-revolving body.

This was the hour of the lizards. Now they had their reward for those days of patient waiting. Plying their sticky pink tongues, they devoured the insects as fast as they came. For hours, they crammed their stomachs, knowing that such a feast would not be theirs again for another year. How wasteful nature is, I thought. Through the whole hot season, the insect world prepares for the flight out of the darkness into light and not one of them survives its freedom.

Suraj and I walked barefooted over the cool, wet pavements, across the railway lines and the riverbed, until we were not far from the crooked tree. Dotting the landscape were old abandoned brick kilns. When it rained heavily, the hollows made by the kilns filled up with water. Suraj and I found a small tank where we could bathe and swim. On a mound in the middle of the tank stood a ruined hut, formerly inhabited by a watchman at the kiln. We swam and then wrestled on the young green grass. Though I was heavier than Suraj and my chest as sound as a new drum, he had a lot of power in his long, wiry arms and legs, and he pinioned me about the waist with his bony knees. And then suddenly, as I strained to press his back to the ground, I felt his body go tense. He stiffened, his thigh jerked against me and his legs began to twitch. I knew that a fit was coming, but I was unable to get out of his grip. He held me more tightly as the fit took possession of him.

When I noticed his mouth working, I thrust the palm of my hand in, sideways, to prevent him from biting his tongue. But so violent was the convulsion that his teeth bit into my flesh. I shouted with pain and tried to pull my hand away, but he was unconscious and his jaw was set. I closed my eyes and counted slowly up to seven and then I felt his muscles relax and I was able to take my hand away. It was bleeding a little but I bound it with a handkerchief before Suraj fully regained consciousness.

He didn't say much as we walked back to town. He looked depressed and weak, but I knew it wouldn't take long for him to recover his usual good spirits. He did not notice that I kept my hand out of sight and only after he had returned from classes that night did he notice the bandage and asked what happened.

X

'Do you want to make some money?' asked Pitamber, bursting into the room like a festive cracker.

'I do,' I said.

'What do we have to do for it?' asked Suraj, striking a cautious note.

'Oh nothing, carry a banner and walk in front of a procession.'

'Why?'

'Don't ask me. Some political stunt.'

'Which party?'

'I don't know. Who cares? All I know is that they are paying two rupees a day to anyone who'll carry a flag or banner.'

'We don't need two rupees that badly,' I said. 'And you can make more than that in a day with your rickshaw.'

'True, but they're paying me *five*. They're fixing a loudspeaker to my rickshaw, and one of the party's men will sit in it and make speeches as we go along. Come on, it will be fun.'

'No banners for us,' I said. 'But we may come along and watch.'

And we did watch, when, later that morning, the procession

passed along our street. It was a ragged procession of about a hundred people, shouting slogans. Some of them were children, and some of them were men who did not know what it was all about, but all joined in the slogan-shouting.

We didn't know much about it, either. Because, though the man in Pitamber's rickshaw was loud and eloquent, his loudspeaker was defective, with the result that his words were punctuated with squeaks and an eerie whining sound. Pitamber looked up and saw us standing on the balcony and gave us a wave and a wide grin. We decided to follow the procession at a discreet distance. It was a protest march against something or other; we never did manage to find out the details. The destination was the municipal office, and by the time we got there, the crowd had increased to two or three hundred people. Some rowdies had now joined in, and things began to get out of hand. The man in the rickshaw continued his speech; another man standing on a wall was making a speech; and someone from the municipal office was confronting the crowd and making a speech of his own.

A stone was thrown, then another. From a sprinkling of stones, it soon became a shower of stones; and then some police constables, who had been standing by watching the fun, were ordered into action. They ran at the crowd where it was thinnest, brandishing stout sticks.

We were caught in the stampede that followed. A stone—flung no doubt at a policeman—was badly aimed and struck me on the shoulder. Suraj pulled me down a side street. Looking back, we saw Pitamber's cycle rickshaw lying on its side in the middle of the road, but there was no sign of Pitamber.

Later, he turned up in my room, with a cut over his left eyebrow which was bleeding freely. Suraj washed the cut, and I poured iodine over it—Pitamber did not flinch—and covered it with sticking plaster. The cut was quite deep and should have had stitches, but Pitamber was superstitious about hospitals, saying he knew very few people to come out of them alive. He was of course thinking about the Pipalnagar hospital.

So he acquired a scar on his forehead. It went rather well with his demonic good looks.

XI

'Thank God for the monsoon,' said Suraj. 'We won't have any more demonstrations on the roads until the weather improves!'

And, until the rain stopped, Pipalnagar was fresh and clean and alive. The children ran naked out of their houses and romped through the streets. The gutters overflowed, and the road became a mountain stream, coursing merrily towards the bus stop.

At the bus stop, there was confusion. Newly arrived passengers, surrounded on all sides by a sea of mud and rainwater, were met by scores of tongas and cycle rickshaws, each jostling the other trying to cater to the passengers. As a result, only half found conveyances, while the other half found themselves knee-deep in Pipalnagar mud.

Pipalnagar mud has a quality all of its own—and it is not easily removed or forgotten. Only buffaloes love it because it is soft and squelchy. Two parts of it are thick, sticky clay which seems to come alive at the slightest touch, clinging tenaciously to human flesh. Feet sink into it and have to be wrenched out. Fingers become webbed. Get it into your hair, and there is nothing you can do except go to Deep Chand and have your head shaved.

London has its fog, Paris its sewers, Pipalnagar its mud.

Pitamber, of course, succeeded in getting as his passenger the most attractive girl to step off the bus, and showed her his skill and daring by taking her to her destination by the longest and roughest road.

The rain swirled over the trees and roofs of the town, and the parched earth soaked it up, giving out a fresh smell that came only once a year, the fragrance of quenched earth, that loveliest of all smells.

In my room, I was battling against the elements, for the door would not close, and the rain swept into the room and soaked my cot. When finally I succeeded in closing the door, I discovered that the roof was leaking and the water was trickling down the walls, running through the dusty design I had made with my feet. I placed tins and mugs in strategic positions and, satisfied that everything was now under control, sat on the cot to watch the rooftops through my windows.

There was a loud banging on the door. It flew open, and there was Suraj standing on the threshold, drenched. Coming in, he began to dry himself while I made desperate efforts to close the door again.

'Let's make some tea,' he said.

Glasses of hot, sweet milky tea on a rainy day...it was enough to make me feel fresh and full of optimism. We sat on the cot, enjoying the brew.

'One day, I'll write a book,' I said. 'Not just a thriller, but a real book, about real people. Perhaps about you and me and Pipalnagar. And then, we'll be famous and our troubles will be over and new troubles will begin. I don't mind problems as long as they are new. While you're studying, I'll write my book. I'll start tonight. It is an auspicious time, the first night of the monsoon.'

A tree must have fallen across the wires somewhere, because the lights would not come on. So I lit a small oil lamp, and while it spluttered in the steamy darkness Suraj opened his book and, with one hand on the book, the other playing with his toe—this helped him to concentrate!—he began to study. I took the inkpot down from the shelf, and finding it empty, added a little rainwater to it from one of the mugs. I sat down beside Suraj and began to write, but the pen was no good and made blotches all over the paper. And, although I was full of writing just then, I didn't really know what I wanted to say.

So I went out and began pacing up and down the road. There I found Pitamber, a little drunk, very merry and prancing about in the middle of the road.

'What are you dancing for?' I asked.

'I'm happy, so I'm dancing,' said Pitamber.

'And why are you happy?' I asked.

'Because I'm dancing,' he said.

The rain stopped and the neem trees gave out a strong, sweet smell.

XII

Flowers in Pipalnagar—did they exist? As a child, I knew a garden in Lucknow where there were beds of phlox and petunias and another garden where only roses grew. In the fields around Pipalnagar was thorn apple—a yellow buttercup nestling among thorn leaves. But in Pipalnagar Bazaar, there were no flowers except one—a marigold growing out of a crack on my balcony. I had removed the plaster from the base of the plant, and filled in a little earth which I watered every morning. The plant was healthy, and sometimes, it produced a small orange marigold.

Sometimes, Suraj plucked a flower and kept it in his tray among the combs, buttons and scent bottles. Sometimes, he gave the flower to a passing child, once to a small boy who immediately tore it to shreds. Suraj was back on his rounds, as his exams were over.

Whenever he was tired of going from house to house, Suraj would sit beneath a shady banyan or peepul tree, put his tray aside and take out his flute. The haunting notes travelled down the road in the afternoon stillness, drawing children to him. They would sit beside him and be very quiet when he played, because there was something melancholic and appealing about the tune. Suraj sometimes made flutes out of pieces of bamboo, but he never sold them. He would give them to the children he liked. He would sell almost anything, but not flutes.

Suraj sometimes played the flute at night, when he lay awake, unable to sleep; but even though I slept, I could hear the music in my dreams. Sometimes, he took his flute with him to the crooked tree and played for the benefit of the birds. The parrots made harsh noises in response and flew away. Once, when Suraj was playing his flute to a small group of children, he had a fit. The flute fell from his hands. And he began to roll about in the dust on the roadside. The children became frightened and ran away, but they did not stay away for long. The next time they heard the flute, they came to listen as usual.

XIII

It was Lord Krishna's birthday, and the rain came down as heavily as it is said to have done on the day he was born. Krishna is the best beloved of all the gods. Young mothers laugh or weep as they read or hear the pranks of his boyhood; young men pray to be as tall and strong as Krishna was when he killed King Kamsa's elephant and wrestlers; young girls dream of a lover as daring as Krishna to carry them off in a war chariot; grown men envy the wisdom and statesmanship with which he managed the affairs of his kingdom.

The rain came so unexpectedly that it took everyone by surprise. In seconds, people were drenched, and within minutes, the streets were flooded. The temple tank overflowed, the railway lines disappeared and the old wall near the bus stop shivered and silently fell—the sound of its collapse drowned in the downpour. A naked young man with a dancing bear cavorted in the middle of the vegetable market. Pitamber's rickshaw churned through the floodwater while he sang lustily as he worked.

Wading through knee-deep water down the road, I saw the roadside vendors salvaging whatever they could. Plastic toys, cabbages and utensils floated away and were seized by urchins. The water had risen to the level of the shop fronts and the floors were awash. Deep Chand and Ramu, with the help of a customer, were using buckets to bail the water out of their shop. The rain stopped as suddenly as it had begun and the sun came out. The water began to find an outlet, flooding other low-lying areas, and a paper boat came sailing between my legs.

Next morning, the morning on which the result of Suraj's examinations was due, I rose early—the first time I ever got up before Suraj—and went down to the news agency. A small crowd of students had gathered at the bus stop, joking with each other and hiding their nervousness with a show of indifference. There were not many passengers on the first bus, and there was a mad grab for newspapers as the bundle landed with a thud on the pavement. Within half-an-hour, the newsboy had sold all his copies. It was the best day of the year for him.

I went through the columns relating to Pipalnagar, but I couldn't find Suraj's roll number on the list of successful candidates. I had the number on a slip of paper, and I looked at it again to make sure I had compared it correctly with the others; then I went through the newspaper once more. When I returned to the room, Suraj was sitting on the doorstep. I didn't have to tell him he had failed—he knew by the look on my face. I sat down beside him, and we said nothing for some time.

'Never mind,' Suraj said eventually. 'I will pass next time.'

I realized I was more depressed than he was and that he was trying to console me.

'If only you'd had more time,' I said.

'I have a year. And you will have time to finish your book, and then we can go away together. Another year of Pipalnagar won't be so bad. As long as I have your friendship, almost everything can be tolerated.'

He stood up, the tray hanging from his shoulders. 'Is there anything you'd like to buy?'

XIV

Another year of Pipalnagar! But it was not to be. A short time later, I received a letter from the editor of a newspaper, calling me to Delhi for an interview. My friends insisted that I should go. Such an opportunity would not come again.

But I needed a shirt. The few I possessed were either frayed at the collar or torn at the shoulders. I hadn't been able to afford a new shirt for over a year, and I couldn't afford one now. Struggling writers weren't expected to dress well, but I felt in order to get the job, I would need both a haircut and a clean shirt.

Where was I to go to get a shirt? Suraj generally wore an old red-striped T-shirt; he washed it every second evening, and by morning, it was dry and ready to wear again; but it was tight even on him. He did not have another. Besides, I needed something white, something respectable!

I went to Deep Chand who had a collection of shirts. He was only too glad to lend me one. But they were all brightly coloured—pinks, purples and magentas... No editor was going to be impressed by a young writer in a pink shirt. They looked fine on Deep Chand, but he had no need to look respectable.

Finally, Pitamber came to my rescue. He didn't bother with shirts himself, except in winter, but he was able to borrow a clean white shirt from a guard at the jail, who'd got it from the relative of a convict in exchange for certain favours.

'This shirt will make you look respectable,' said Pitamber. 'To be respectable—what an adventure!'

XV

Freedom. The moment the bus was out of Pipalnagar and the fields opened out on all sides, I knew that I was free, that I had always been free. Only my own weakness, hesitation and the habits that had grown around me had held me back. All I had to do was sit in a bus and go somewhere.

I sat near the open window of the bus and let the cool breeze from the fields play against my face. Herons and snipe waded among the lotus roots in flat green ponds. Blue jays swooped around telegraph poles. Children jumped naked into the canals that wound through the fields. Because I was happy, it seemed to me that everyone else was happy—the driver, the conductor, the passengers, the farmers in the fields and those driving bullock carts. When two women behind me started quarrelling over their seats, I helped to placate them. Then I took a small girl on my knee and pointed out camels, buffaloes, vultures and pariah dogs.

Six hours later, the bus crossed the bridge over the swollen Yamuna River, passed under the walls of the great Red Fort built by a Mughal emperor and entered the old city of Delhi. I found it strange to be in a city again, after several years in Pipalnagar. It was a little frightening too. I felt like a stranger. No one was interested in me.

In Pipalnagar, people wanted to know each other, or at least to know about one another. In Delhi, no one cared who you were or where you came from, like big cities almost everywhere. It was prosperous but without a heart.

After a day and a night of loneliness, I found myself wishing that Suraj had accompanied me; wishing that I was back in Pipalnagar. But when the job was offered to me—at a starting salary of three hundred rupees per month, a princely sum compared to what I had been making on my own—I did not have the courage to refuse it. After accepting the job—which was to commence in a week's time—I spent the day wandering through the bazaars, down the wide, shady roads of the capital, resting under the jamun trees and thinking all the time what I would do in the months to come.

I slept at the railway waiting room, and all night long, I heard the shunting and whistling of engines which conjured up visions of places with sweet names like Kumbakonam, Krishnagiri, Polonnarurawa. I dreamt of palm-fringed beaches and inland lagoons; of the echoing chambers of deserted cities, red sandstone and white marble; of temples in the sun; and elephants crossing wide, slow-moving rivers...

XVI

Pitamber was on the platform when the train steamed into the Pipalnagar station in the early hours of a damp September morning. I waved to him from the carriage window and shouted that everything had gone well.

But everything was not well here. When I got off the train, Pitamber told me that Suraj had been ill—that he'd had a fit on a lonely stretch of road the previous afternoon and had lain in the sun for over an hour. Pitamber had found him, suffering from heatstroke and brought him home. When I saw him, he was sitting up on the string bed drinking hot tea. He looked pale and weak, but his smile was reassuring.

'Don't worry,' he said. 'I will be all right.'

'He was bad last night,' said Pitamber. 'He had a fever and kept talking, as in a dream. But what he says is true—he is better this morning.'

'Thanks to Pitamber,' said Suraj. 'It is good to have friends.'

'Come with me to Delhi, Suraj,' I said. 'I have got a job now. You can live with me and attend a school regularly.'

'It is good for friends to help each other,' said Suraj, 'but only after I have passed my exam will I join you in Delhi. I made myself this promise. Poor Pipalnagar—nobody wants to stay here. Will you be sorry to leave?'

'Yes, I will be sorry. A part of me will still be here.'

XVII

Deep Chand was happy to know that I was leaving. 'I'll follow you soon,' he said. 'There is money to be made in Delhi, cutting hair. Girls are keeping it short these days.'

'But men are growing it long.'

'True. So I shall open a barber shop for ladies and a beauty salon for men! Ramu can attend to the ladies.'

Ramu winked at me in the mirror. He was still at the stage of teasing girls on their way to school or college.

The snip of Deep Chand's scissors made me sleepy, as I sat in his chair. His fingers beat a rhythmic tattoo on my scalp. It was my last haircut in Pipalnagar, and Deep Chand did not charge me for it. I promised to write as soon as I had settled down in Delhi.

The next day when Suraj was stronger, I said, 'Come, let us go for a walk and visit our crooked tree. Where is your flute, Suraj?'

'I don't know. Let us look for it.'

We searched the room and our belongings for the flute but could not find it.

'It must have been left on the roadside,' said Suraj. 'Never mind. I will make another.'

I could picture the flute lying in the dust on the roadside and somehow this made me sad. But Suraj was full of high spirits as we walked across the railway lines and through the fields.

'The rains are over,' he said, kicking off his chappals and lying down on the grass. 'You can smell the autumn in the air. Somehow, it makes me feel light-hearted. Yesterday I was sad, and tomorrow I might be sad again, but today I know that I am happy. I want to live on and on. One lifetime cannot satisfy my heart.'

'A day in a lifetime,' I said. 'I'll remember this day—the way the sun touches us, the way the grass bends, the smell of this leaf as I crush it...'

XVIII

Every morning at six, the first bus arrives, and the passengers alight, looking sleepy and dishevelled and rather discouraged by their first sight of Pipalnagar. When they have gone their various ways, the bus is driven into the shed. Cows congregate at the dustbin and the pavement dwellers come to life, stretching their tired limbs on the hard stone steps. I carry the bucket up the steps to my room and bathe for the last time on the open balcony. In the villages, the buffaloes are wallowing in green ponds while naked urchins sit astride them, scrubbing their backs, and a crow or water bird perches on their glistening necks. The parrots are busy in the crooked tree, and a slim green snake basks in the sun on our island near the brick kiln. In the hills, the mists have lifted and the distant mountains are fringed with snow.

It is autumn, and the rains are over. The earth meets the sky in one broad, bold sweep.

A land of thrusting hills. Terraced hills, wood-covered and windswept. Mountains where the gods speak gently to the lonely. Hills of green grass and grey rock, misty at dawn, hazy at noon, molten at sunset, where fierce, fresh torrents rush to the valleys below. A quiet land of fields and ponds, shaded by ancient trees and ringed with palms, where sacred rivers are touched by temples, where temples are touched by southern seas.

This is the land I should write about. Pipalnagar should be forgotten. I should turn aside from it to sing instead of the splendours of exotic places.

But only yesterdays are truly splendid... And there are other singers, sweeter than I, to sing of tomorrow. I can only write of today, of Pipalnagar, where I have lived and loved.

A LONG WALK FOR BINA

I

A leopard, lithe and sinewy, drank at the mountain stream, and then lay down on the grass to bask in the late February sunshine. Its tail twitched occasionally and the animal appeared to be sleeping. At the sound of distant voices, it raised its head to listen, then stood up and leapt lightly over the boulders in the stream, disappearing among the trees on the opposite bank.

A minute or two later, three children came walking down the forest path. They were a girl and two boys, and they were singing in their local dialect an old song they had learnt from their grandparents.

> Five more miles to go!
> We climb through rain and snow.
> A river to cross...
> A mountain to pass...
> Now we've four more miles to go!

Their school satchels looked new, their clothes had been washed and pressed. Their loud and cheerful singing startled a spotted forktail. The bird left its favourite rock in the stream and flew down the dark ravine.

'Well, we have only three more miles to go,' said the bigger boy, Prakash, who had been this way hundreds of times. 'But first, we have to cross the stream.'

He was a sturdy twelve-year-old with eyes like black currants and a mop of bushy hair that refused to settle down on his head. The girl and her small brother were taking this path for the first time.

'I'm feeling tired, Bina,' said the little boy.

Bina smiled at him, and Prakash said, 'Don't worry, Sonu, you'll get used to the walk. There's plenty of time.' He glanced at the old watch he'd been given by his grandfather. It needed constant winding. 'We can rest here for five or six minutes.'

They sat down on a smooth boulder and watched the clear water of the shallow stream tumbling downhill. Bina examined the old watch on Prakash's wrist. The glass was badly scratched and she could barely make out the figures on the dial. 'Are you sure it still gives the right time?' she asked.

'Well, it loses five minutes every day, so I put it ten minutes ahead at night. That means by morning it's quite accurate! Even our teacher, Mr Mani, asks me for the time. If he doesn't ask, I tell him! The clock in our classroom keeps stopping.'

They removed their shoes and let the cold mountain water run over their feet. Bina was the same age as Prakash. She had pink cheeks, soft brown eyes and hair that was just beginning to lose its natural curls. Hers was a gentle face, but a determined little chin showed that she could be a strong person. Sonu, her younger brother, was ten. He was a thin boy who had been sickly as a child but was now beginning to fill out. Although he did not look very athletic, he could run like the wind.

◆

Bina had been going to school in her own village of Koli, on the other side of the mountain. But it had been a primary school, finishing at Class 5. Now, in order to study in Class 6, she would have to walk several miles every day to Nauti, where there was a high school going up to Class 8. It had been decided that Sonu would also shift to the new school, to give Bina company. Prakash, their neighbour in Koli, was already a pupil at the Nauti school. His mischievous nature, which sometimes got him into trouble, had resulted in his having to repeat a year.

But this didn't seem to bother him. 'What's the hurry?' he had told his indignant parents. 'You're not sending me to a foreign land when I finish school. And our cows aren't running away, are they?'

'You would prefer to look after the cows, wouldn't you?' asked Bina, as they got up to continue their walk.

'Oh, school's all right. Wait till you see old Mr Mani. He always gets our names mixed up, as well as the subjects he's supposed to be teaching. At our last lesson, instead of maths, he gave us a geography lesson!'

'More fun than maths,' said Bina.

'Yes, but there's a new teacher this year. She's very young they say, just out of college. I wonder what she'll be like.'

Bina walked faster and Sonu had some trouble keeping up with them. She was excited about the new school and the prospect of different surroundings. She had seldom been outside her own village, with its small school and single ration shop. The day's routine never varied—helping her mother in the fields or with household tasks like fetching water from the spring or cutting grass and fodder for the cattle. Her father, who was a soldier, was away for nine months in the year, and Sonu was still too small for the heavier tasks.

As they neared Nauti Village, they were joined by other children coming from different directions. Even where there were no major roads, the mountains were full of little lanes and shortcuts. Like a game of snakes and ladders, these narrow paths zigzagged around the hills and villages, cutting through fields and crossing narrow ravines until they came together to form a fairly busy road along which mules, cattle and goats joined the throng.

Nauti was a fairly large village, and from here, a broader but dustier road started for Tehri. There was a small bus, several trucks and (for part of the way) a road roller. The road hadn't been completed because the heavy diesel roller couldn't take the steep climb to Nauti. It stood on the roadside halfway up the road from Tehri.

Prakash knew almost everyone in the area and exchanged greetings and gossip with other children as well as with muleteers, bus drivers, milkmen and labourers working on the road. He loved telling everyone the time, even if they weren't interested.

'It's nine o'clock,' he would announce, glancing at his wrist. 'Isn't your bus leaving today?'

'Off with you!' the bus driver would respond, 'I'll leave when I'm ready.'

As the children approached Nauti, the small flat school buildings came into view on the outskirts of the village, fringed by a line of long-leaved pines. A small crowd had assembled on the one playing field. Something unusual seemed to have happened. Prakash ran forward to see what it was all about. Bina and Sonu stood aside, waiting in a patch of sunlight near the boundary wall.

Prakash soon came running back to them. He was bubbling over with excitement.

'It's Mr Mani!' he gasped. 'He's disappeared! People are saying a leopard must have carried him off!'

II

Mr Mani wasn't really old. He was about fifty-five and was expected to retire soon. But for the children, most adults over forty seemed ancient! And Mr Mani had always been a bit absent-minded, even as a young man.

He had gone out for his early morning walk, saying he'd be back by eight o'clock, in time to have his breakfast and be ready for class. He wasn't married, but his sister and her husband stayed with him. When it was past nine o'clock, his sister presumed he'd stopped at a neighbour's house for breakfast (he loved tucking into other people's breakfast) and that he had gone on to school from there. But when the school bell rang at ten o'clock, and everyone but Mr Mani was present, questions were asked and guesses were made.

No one had seen him return from his walk and enquiries made in the village showed that he had not stopped at anyone's house. For Mr Mani to disappear was puzzling; for him to disappear without his breakfast was extraordinary.

Then a milkman returning from the next village said he had seen a leopard sitting on a rock on the outskirts of the pine forest. There had been talk of a cattle-killer in the valley, of leopards and other animals being displaced by the construction of a dam. But as yet, no one had heard of a leopard attacking a man. Could Mr Mani have been its first victim? Someone found a strip of red cloth entangled in a blackberry bush and went running through the village showing it to everyone. Mr Mani had been known to wear red pyjamas. Surely, he had been seized and eaten! But where were his remains? And why had he been in his pyjamas?

Meanwhile, Bina and Sonu and the rest of the children had

followed their teachers into the school playground. Feeling a little lost, Bina looked around for Prakash. She found herself facing a dark, slender young woman wearing spectacles, who must have been in her early twenties—just a little too old to be another student. She had a kind, expressive face and she seemed a little concerned by all that had been happening.

Bina noticed that she had lovely hands; it was obvious that the new teacher hadn't milked cows or worked in the fields!

'You must be new here,' said the teacher, smiling at Bina. 'And is this your little brother?'

'Yes, we've come from Koli Village. We were at school there.'

'It's a long walk from Koli. You didn't see any leopards, did you? Well, I'm new too. Are you in the sixth class?'

'Sonu is in the third. I'm in the sixth.'

'Then I'm your new teacher. My name is Tania Ramola. Come along, let's see if we can settle down in our classroom.'

♦

Mr Mani turned up at twelve o'clock, wondering what all the fuss was about. No, he snapped, he had not been attacked by a leopard; and yes, he had lost his pyjamas and would someone kindly return them to him?

'How did you lose your pyjamas, sir?' asked Prakash.

'They were blown off the washing line!' snapped Mr Mani.

After much questioning, Mr Mani admitted that he had gone further than he had intended, and that he had lost his way coming back. He had been a bit upset because the new teacher, a slip of a girl, had been given charge of the sixth, while he was still with the fifth, along with that troublesome boy Prakash, who kept on reminding him of the time! The Headmaster had explained that as Mr Mani was due to retire at the end of the year, the school did not wish to burden him with a senior class. But Mr Mani looked upon the whole thing as a plot to get rid of him. He glowered at Miss Ramola whenever he passed her. And when she smiled back at him, he looked the other way!

Mr Mani had been getting even more absent-minded of late—putting on his shoes without his socks, wearing his homespun waistcoat inside out, mixing up people's names and, of course, eating other people's lunches and dinners. His sister had made a mutton broth for the postmaster, who was down with 'flu', and had asked Mr Mani to take it over in a thermos. When the postmaster opened the thermos, he found only a few drops of broth at the bottom—Mr Mani had drunk the rest somewhere along the way.

When sometimes Mr Mani spoke of his coming retirement, it was to describe his plans for the small field he owned just behind the house. Right now, it was full of potatoes, which did not require much looking after; but he had plans for growing dahlias, roses, French beans, and other fruits and flowers.

The next time he visited Tehri, he promised himself, he would buy some dahlia bulbs and rose cuttings. The monsoon season would be a good time to put them down. And meanwhile, his potatoes were still flourishing.

III

Bina enjoyed her first day at the new school. She felt at ease with Miss Ramola, as did most of the boys and girls in her class. Tania Ramola had been to distant towns such as Delhi and Lucknow—places they had only heard about—and it was said that she had a brother who was a pilot and flew planes all over the world. Perhaps, he'd fly over Nauti some day!

Most of the children had of course seen planes flying overhead, but none of them had seen a ship, and only a few had been on a train. Tehri mountain was far from the railway and hundreds of miles from the sea. But they all knew about the big dam that was being built at Tehri, just forty miles away.

Bina, Sonu and Prakash had company for part of the way home, but gradually, the other children went off in different directions. Once they had crossed the stream, they were on their own again.

It was a steep climb all the way back to their village. Prakash had a supply of peanuts which he shared with Bina and Sonu, and at a small spring, they quenched their thirst.

When they were less than a mile from home, they met a postman who had finished his round of the villages in the area and was now returning to Nauti.

'Don't waste time along the way,' he told them. 'Try to get home before dark.'

'What's the hurry?' asked Prakash, glancing at his watch. 'It's only five o'clock.'

'There's a leopard around. I saw it this morning, not far from the stream. No one is sure how it got here. So don't take any chances. Get home early.'

'So, there really is a leopard,' said Sonu.

They took his advice and walked faster, and Sonu forgot to complain about his aching feet.

They were home well before sunset.

There was a smell of cooking in the air and they were hungry.

'Cabbage and roti,' said Prakash gloomily. 'But I could eat anything today.' He stopped outside his small slate-roofed house, and Bina and Sonu waved goodbye and carried on across a couple of ploughed fields until they reached their small stone house.

'Stuffed tomatoes,' said Sonu, sniffing just outside the front door.

'And lemon pickle,' said Bina, who had helped cut, sun and salt the lemons a month previously.

Their mother was lighting the kitchen stove. They greeted her with great hugs and demands for an immediate dinner. She was a good cook who could make even the simplest of dishes taste delicious. Her favourite saying was, 'Home-made bread is better than roast meat abroad,' and Bina and Sonu had to agree.

Electricity had yet to reach their village, and they took their meal by the light of a kerosene lamp. After the meal, Sonu settled down to do a little homework, while Bina stepped outside to look at the stars.

Across the fields, someone was playing a flute. 'It must be Prakash,' thought Bina. 'He always breaks off on the high notes.' But the flute music was simple and appealing, and she began singing softly to herself in the dark.

IV

Mr Mani was having trouble with the porcupines. They had been getting into his garden at night and digging up and eating his potatoes. From his bedroom window—left open now that the mild April weather had arrived—he could listen to them enjoying the vegetables he had worked hard to grow. Scrunch, scrunch! katar, katar, as their sharp teeth sliced through the largest and juiciest of potatoes. For Mr Mani it was as though they were biting through his own flesh. And the sound of them digging industriously as they rooted up those healthy, leafy plants made him tremble with rage and indignation. The unfairness of it all!

Yes, Mr Mani hated porcupines. He prayed for their

destruction, their removal from the face of the earth. But, as his friends were quick to point out, 'The creator made porcupines too,' and in any case you could never see the creatures or catch them, they were completely nocturnal.

Mr Mani got out of bed every night, torch in one hand, a stout stick in the other but, as soon as he stepped into the garden, the crunching and digging stopped and he was greeted by the most infuriating of silences. He would grope around in the dark, swinging wildly with the stick, but not a single porcupine was to be seen or heard. As soon as he was back in bed, the sounds would start all over again—scrunch, scrunch, katar, katar...

Mr Mani came to his class tired and dishevelled, with rings under his eyes and a permanent frown on his face. It took some time for his pupils to discover the reason for his misery, but when they did, they felt sorry for their teacher and took to discussing ways and means of saving his potatoes from the porcupines.

It was Prakash who came up with the idea of a moat or water ditch. 'Porcupines don't like water,' he said knowledgeably.

'How do you know?' asked one of his friends.

'Throw water on one and see how it runs! They don't like getting their quills wet.'

There was no one who could disprove Prakash's theory, and the class fell in with the idea of building a moat, especially as it meant getting most of the day off.

'Anything to make Mr Mani happy,' said the Headmaster, and the rest of the school watched with envy as the pupils of Class 5, armed with spades and shovels collected from all parts of the village, took up their positions around Mr Mani's potato field and began digging a ditch.

By evening the moat was ready, but it was still dry and the porcupines got in again that night and had a great feast.

'At this rate,' said Mr Mani gloomily, 'there won't be any potatoes left to save.'

But the next day, Prakash and the other boys and girls managed to divert the water from a stream that flowed past the village. They had the satisfaction of watching it flow gently into the ditch. Everyone went home in a good mood. By nightfall, the ditch had overflowed, the potato field was flooded, and Mr Mani found himself trapped inside his house. But Prakash and his friends had won the day. The porcupines stayed away that night!

◆

A month had passed, and wild violets, daisies and buttercups now sprinkled the hill slopes and, on her way to school, Bina gathered enough to make a little posy. The bunch of flowers fitted easily into an old ink well. Miss Ramola was delighted to find this little display in the middle of her desk.

'Who put these here?' she asked in surprise.

Bina kept quiet, and the rest of the class smiled secretively. After that, they took turns bringing flowers for the classroom.

On her long walks to school and home again, Bina became aware that April was the month of new leaves. The oak leaves were bright green above and silver beneath, and when they rippled in the breeze, they were clouds of silvery green. The path was strewn with old leaves, dry and crackly. Sonu loved kicking them around.

Clouds of white butterflies floated across the stream. Sonu was chasing a butterfly when he stumbled over something dark and repulsive. He went sprawling on the grass. When he got to his feet, he looked down at the remains of a small animal.

'Bina! Prakash! Come quickly!' he shouted.

It was part of a sheep, killed some days earlier by a much larger animal.

'Only a leopard could have done this,' said Prakash.

'Let's get away, then,' said Sonu. 'It might still be around!'

'No, there's nothing left to eat. The leopard will be hunting elsewhere by now. Perhaps, it's moved on to the next valley.'

'Still, I'm frightened,' said Sonu. 'There may be more leopards!'

Bina took him by the hand. 'Leopards don't attack humans!' she said.

'They will, if they get a taste for people!' insisted Prakash.

'Well, this one hasn't attacked any people as yet,' said Bina, although she couldn't be sure. Hadn't there been rumours of a leopard attacking some workers near the dam? But she did not want Sonu to feel afraid, so she did not mention the story. All she said was, 'It has probably come here because of all the activity near the dam.'

All the same, they hurried home. And for a few days, whenever they reached the stream, they crossed over very quickly, unwilling to linger too long at that lovely spot.

V

A few days later, a school party was on its way to Tehri to see the new dam that was being built.

Miss Ramola had arranged to take her class, and Mr Mani, not wishing to be left out, insisted on taking his class as well. That meant there were about fifty boys and girls taking part in the outing. The little bus could only take thirty. A friendly truck driver agreed to take some children if they were prepared to sit on sacks of potatoes. And Prakash persuaded the owner of the diesel roller to turn it around and head it back to Tehri—with him and a couple of friends up on the driving seat.

Prakash's small group set off at sunrise, as they had to walk some distance in order to reach the stranded road roller. The bus left at 9 a.m. with Miss Ramola and her class, and Mr Mani and some of his pupils. The truck was to follow later.

It was Bina's first visit to a large town and her first bus ride.

The sharp curves along the winding, downhill road made several children feel sick. The bus driver seemed to be in a tearing hurry. He took them along at a rolling, rollicking speed, which made Bina feel quite giddy. She rested her head on her arms and refused to look out of the window. Hairpin bends and cliff edges, pine forests and snow-capped peaks, all swept past her, but she felt too ill to want to look at anything. It was just as well—those sudden drops, hundreds of feet to the valley below, were quite frightening. Bina began to wish that she hadn't come—or that she had joined Prakash on the road roller instead!

Miss Ramola and Mr Mani didn't seem to notice the lurching and groaning of the old bus. They had made this journey many times. They were busy arguing about the advantages and disadvantages of large dams—an argument that was to continue on and off for much of the day.

Meanwhile, Prakash and his friends had reached the roller. The driver hadn't turned up, but they managed to reverse it and get it going in the direction of Tehri. They were soon overtaken by both bus and truck but kept moving along at a steady chug. Prakash spotted Bina at the window of the bus and waved cheerfully. She responded feebly.

Bina felt better when the road levelled out near Tehri. As they crossed an old bridge over the wide river, they were startled by a loud bang which made the bus shudder. A cloud of dust rose above the town.

'They're blasting the mountain,' said Miss Ramola.

'End of a mountain,' said Mr Mani, mournfully.

While they were drinking cups of tea at the bus stop, waiting for the potato truck and the road roller, Miss Ramola and Mr Mani continued their argument about the dam. Miss Ramola maintained that it would bring electric power and water for irrigation to large areas of the country, including the surrounding area. Mr Mani declared that it was a menace, as it was situated in an earthquake zone. There would be a terrible disaster if the dam burst! Bina found it all very confusing. And what about the animals in the area, she wondered, what would happen to them?

The argument was becoming quite heated when the potato truck arrived. There was no sign of the road roller, so it was decided that Mr Mani should wait for Prakash and his friends while Miss Ramola's group went ahead.

◆

Some eight or nine miles before Tehri, the road roller had broken down, and Prakash and his friends were forced to walk. They had not gone far, however, when a mule train came along—five or six mules that had been delivering sacks of grain in Nauti. A boy rode on the first mule, but the others had no loads.

'Can you give us a ride to Tehri?' called Prakash.

'Make yourselves comfortable,' said the boy.

There were no saddles, only gunny sacks strapped on to the mules with rope. They had a rough but jolly ride down to the Tehri bus stop. None of them had ever ridden mules; but they had saved at least an hour on the road.

Looking around the bus stop for the rest of the party, they could find no one from their school. And Mr Mani, who should have been waiting for them, had vanished.

VI

Tania Ramola and her group had taken the steep road to the hill above Tehri. Half an hour's climbing brought them to a little plateau which overlooked the town, the river and the dam site.

The earthworks for the dam were only just coming up, but a wide tunnel had been bored through the mountain to divert the river into another channel. Down below, the old town was still spread out across the valley and from a distance it looked quite charming and picturesque.

'Will the whole town be swallowed up by the waters of the dam?' asked Bina.

'Yes, all of it,' said Miss Ramola. 'The clock tower and the old palace. The long bazaar and the temples, the schools and the jail, and hundreds of houses, for many miles up the valley. All those people will have to go—thousands of them! Of course, they'll be resettled elsewhere.'

'But the town's been here for hundreds of years,' said Bina. 'They were quite happy without the dam, weren't they?'

'I suppose they were. But the dam isn't just for them—it's for the millions who live further downstream, across the plains.'

'And it doesn't matter what happens to this place?'

'The local people will be given new homes somewhere else.' Miss Ramola found herself on the defensive and decided to change the subject. 'Everyone must be hungry. It's time we had our lunch.'

Bina kept quiet. She didn't think the local people would want to go away. And it was a good thing, she mused, that there was only a small stream and not a big river running past her village. To be uprooted like this—a town and hundreds of villages—and put down somewhere on the hot, dusty plains—seemed to her unbearable.

'Well, I'm glad I don't live in Tehri,' she said.

She did not know it, but all the animals and most of the birds had already left the area. The leopard had been among them.

◆

They walked through the colourful, crowded bazaar, where fruit sellers did business beside silversmiths, and pavement vendors sold everything from umbrellas to glass bangles. Sparrows attacked sacks of grain, monkeys made off with bananas and stray cows and dogs rummaged in refuse bins, but nobody took any notice. Music blared from radios. Buses blew their horns. Sonu bought a whistle to add to the general din, but Miss Ramola told him to put it away. Bina had kept five rupees aside, and now she used it to buy a cotton headscarf for her mother.

As they were about to enter a small restaurant for a meal, they were joined by Prakash and his companions; but of Mr Mani there was still no sign.

'He must have met one of his relatives,' said Prakash. 'He has relatives everywhere.'

After a simple meal of rice and lentils, they walked the length of the bazaar without finding Mr Mani. At last, when they were about to give up the search, they saw him emerge from a by-lane, a large sack slung over his shoulder.

'Sir, where have you been?' asked Prakash. 'We have been looking for you everywhere.'

On Mr Mani's face was a look of triumph.
'Help me with this bag,' he said breathlessly.
'You've bought more potatoes, sir,' said Prakash.
'Not potatoes, boy. Dahlia bulbs!'

VII

It was dark by the time they were all back in Nauti. Mr Mani had refused to be separated from his sack of dahlia bulbs and had been forced to sit in the back of the truck with Prakash and most of the boys.

Bina did not feel so ill on the return journey. Going uphill was definitely better than going downhill! But by the time the bus reached Nauti, it was too late for most of the children to walk back to the more distant villages. The boys were put up in different homes while the girls were given beds in the school veranda.

The night was warm and still. Large moths fluttered around the single bulb that lit the veranda. Counting moths, Sonu soon fell asleep. But Bina stayed awake for some time, listening to the sounds of the night. A nightjar went tonk-tonk in the bushes, and somewhere in the forest an owl hooted softly. The sharp call of a barking deer travelled up the valley from the direction of the stream. Jackals kept howling. It seemed that there were more of them than ever before.

Bina was not the only one to hear the barking deer. The leopard, stretched full length on a rocky ledge, heard it too. The leopard raised its head and then got up slowly. The deer was its natural prey. But there weren't many left, and that was why the leopard, robbed of its forest by the dam, had taken to attacking dogs and cattle near the villages.

As the cry of the barking deer sounded nearer, the leopard left its lookout point and moved swiftly through the shadows towards the stream.

VIII

In early June, the hills were dry and dusty, and forest fires broke out, destroying shrubs and trees, killing birds and small animals. The resin in the pines made these trees burn more fiercely, and the wind would take sparks from the trees and carry them into the dry grass and leaves so that new fires would spring up before the old ones had died out. Fortunately, Bina's village was not in the pine belt; the fires did not reach it. But Nauti was surrounded by a fire that raged for three days, and the children had to stay away from school.

And then, towards the end of June, the monsoon rains arrived and there was an end to forest fires. The monsoon lasts three months and the lower Himalayas would be drenched in rain, mist and cloud for the next three months.

The first rain arrived while Bina, Prakash and Sonu were returning home from school. Those first few drops on the dusty path made them cry out with excitement. Then the rain grew heavier and a wonderful aroma rose from the earth.

'The best smell in the world!' exclaimed Bina.

Everything suddenly came to life. The grass, the crops, the trees, the birds. Even the leaves of the trees glistened and looked new.

That first wet weekend, Bina and Sonu helped their mother plant beans, maize and cucumbers. Sometimes, when the rain was very heavy, they had to run indoors. Otherwise, they worked in the rain, the soft mud clinging to their bare legs.

Prakash now owned a dog, a black dog with one ear up and one ear down. The dog ran around getting in everyone's way, barking at cows, goats, hens and humans, without frightening any of them. Prakash said it was a very clever dog, but no one else seemed to think so. Prakash also said it would protect the village from the leopard, but others said the dog would be the first to be taken—he'd run straight into the jaws of Mr Spots!

In Nauti, Tania Ramola was trying to find a dry spot in the quarters she'd been given. It was an old building and the roof was leaking in several places. Mugs and buckets were scattered about the floor in order to catch the drips.

Mr Mani had dug up all his potatoes and presented them to the friends and neighbours who had given him lunches and dinners. He was having the time of his life, planting dahlia bulbs all over his garden.

'I'll have a field of many-coloured dahlias!' he announced. 'Just wait till the end of August!'

'Watch out for those porcupines,' warned his sister. 'They eat dahlia bulbs too!'

Mr Mani made an inspection tour of his moat, no longer in flood, and found everything in good order. Prakash had done his job well.

◆

Now, when the children crossed the stream, they found that the water level had risen by about a foot. Small cascades had turned into waterfalls. Ferns had sprung up on the banks. Frogs chanted.

Prakash and his dog dashed across the stream. Bina and Sonu followed more cautiously. The current was much stronger now and the water was almost up to their knees. Once they had crossed the stream, they hurried along the path, anxious not to be caught in a sudden downpour.

By the time they reached school, each of them had two or three leeches clinging to their legs. They had to use salt to remove them. The leeches were the most troublesome part of the rainy season. Even the leopard did not like them. It could not lie in the long grass without getting leeches on its paws and face.

One day, when Bina, Prakash and Sonu were about to cross the stream they heard a low rumble, which grew louder every second. Looking up at the opposite hill, they saw several trees shudder, tilt outwards and begin to fall. Earth and rocks bulged out from the mountain, then came crashing down into the ravine.

'Landslide!' shouted Sonu.

'It's carried away the path,' said Bina. 'Don't go any further.'

There was a tremendous roar as more rocks, trees and bushes fell away and crashed down the hillside.

Prakash's dog, who had gone ahead, came running back, tail between his legs.

They remained rooted to the spot until the rocks had stopped falling and the dust had settled. Birds circled the area, calling wildly. A frightened barking deer ran past them.

'We can't go to school now,' said Prakash. 'There's no way around.'

They turned and trudged home through the gathering mist.

In Koli, Prakash's parents had heard the roar of the landslide. They were setting out in search of the children when they saw them emerge from the mist, waving cheerfully.

IX

They had to miss school for another three days, and Bina was afraid they might not be able to take their final exams. Although Prakash was not really troubled at the thought of missing exams, he did not like feeling helpless just because their path had been swept away. So he explored the hillside until he found a goat-track going around the mountain. It joined up with another path near Nauti. This made their walk longer by a mile, but Bina did not mind. It was much cooler now that the rains were in full swing.

The only trouble with the new route was that it passed close to the leopard's lair. The animal had made this area its own since being forced to leave the dam area.

One day, Prakash's dog ran ahead of them barking furiously. Then he ran back whimpering.

'He's always running away from something,' observed Sonu. But a minute later, he understood the reason for the dog's fear.

They rounded a bend and Sonu saw the leopard standing in their way. They were struck dumb—too terrified to run. It was a strong, sinewy creature. A low growl rose from its throat. It seemed ready to spring.

They stood perfectly still, afraid to move or say a word. And the leopard must have been equally surprised. It stared at them for a few seconds, then bounded across the path and into the oak forest.

Sonu was shaking. Bina could hear her heart hammering. Prakash could only stammer: 'Did you see the way he sprang? Wasn't he beautiful?'

He forgot to look at his watch for the rest of the day.

A few days later, Sonu stopped and pointed to a large

outcrop of rock on the next hill.

The leopard stood far above them, outlined against the sky. It looked strong, majestic. Standing beside it were two young cubs.

'Look at those little ones!' exclaimed Sonu.

'So it's a female, not a male,' said Prakash.

'That's why she was killing so often,' said Bina. 'She had to feed her cubs too.'

They remained still for several minutes, gazing up at the leopard and her cubs. The leopard family took no notice of them.

'She knows we are here,' said Prakash, 'but she doesn't care. She knows we won't harm them.'

'We are cubs too!' said Sonu.

'Yes,' said Bina. 'And there's still plenty of space for all of us. Even when the dam is ready there will still be room for leopards and humans.'

X

The school exams were over. The rains were nearly over too. The landslide had been cleared, and Bina, Prakash and Sonu were once again crossing the stream.

There was a chill in the air, for it was the end of September.

Prakash had learnt to play the flute quite well, and he played on the way to school and then again on the way home. As a result, he did not look at his watch so often. One morning, they found a small crowd in front of Mr Mani's house.

'What could have happened?' wondered Bina. 'I hope he hasn't got lost again.'

'Maybe he's sick,' said Sonu.

'Maybe it's the porcupines,' said Prakash.

But it was none of these things.

Mr Mani's first dahlia was in bloom, and half the village had turned up to look at it! It was a huge red double dahlia, so heavy that it had to be supported with sticks. No one had ever seen such a magnificent flower!

Mr Mani was a happy man. And his mood only improved over the coming week as more and more dahlias flowered—crimson, yellow, purple, mauve, white—button dahlias, pom-pom dahlias, spotted dahlias, striped dahlias... Mr Mani had them all! A dahlia even turned up on Tania Ramola's desk—he got along quite well with her now—and another brightened up the Headmaster's study.

A week later, on their way home—it was almost the last day of the school term—Bina, Prakash and Sonu talked about what they might do when they grew up.

'I think I'll become a teacher,' said Bina. 'I'll teach children about animals and birds, and trees and flowers.'

'Better than maths!' said Prakash.

'I'll be a pilot,' said Sonu. 'I want to fly a plane like Miss Ramola's brother.'

'And what about you, Prakash?' asked Bina.

Prakash just smiled and said, 'Maybe I'll be a flute player,' and he put the flute to his lips and played a sweet melody.

'Well, the world needs flute players too,' said Bina, as they fell into step beside him.

The leopard had been stalking a barking deer. She paused when she heard the flute and the voices of the children. Her own young ones were growing quickly, but the girl and the two boys did not look much older.

They had started singing their favourite song again.

> Five more miles to go!
> We climb through rain and snow,
> A river to cross...
> A mountain to pass...
> Now we've four more miles to go!

The leopard waited until they had passed, before returning to the trail of the barking deer.